21 Days

A lockdown story

by
Albert Gumbo

© Albert Gumbo 2020

Twenty-one Days

Published by Oyster Consulting

Paulshof, South Africa

gumbo.albert@gmail.com

ISBN 978-0-620-89257-5

2 4 6 8 10 9 7 5 3 1

Layout and cover design by Boutique Books

To Li Wenliang

Thaba Patchoa crawled into the plastic and cardboard shack and said to his wife, "I hear the president is going to talk to the whole country".

"Why?" His wife carefully moved to the side so that he could fit in and not squash their two-year-old in their tiny dwelling.

"Something about this new disease that is scaring white people."

Thaba worked at the local barbershop in Twinstreams, a leafy suburb in Johannesburg's northern area. His job was to sweep the floor after every customer had had their hair cut and he listened to a lot of conversations.

"Hai! These white people are excitable," replied his wife, adding, "They even get the president to say something about it."

She moved carefully, not letting her kanga slip. The moment she let her thighs show, Thaba might get ideas and she was not in the mood. She was tired from spending all day chasing after her two-year-old to stop him from venturing too close to the stream. They lived illegally on a piece of land where two streams met before flowing away on one journey, Thaba said, to the Indian Ocean. His wife used to roll her eyes at this absurdity. She remembered from a distant, short-lived Geography lesson that India was quite far away. There was no way this little stream would make it all the way there.

To their left, across one of the streams, was a stable where rich housewives came and watched their children riding horses in the afternoons during the week and all day on weekends. They had moved to this spot from Bloemfontein, four hundred kilometres away, a town they considered part of their homeland of Lesotho. Crossing the border back and forth, at a crossing point of their choosing, was the norm to them. Their grandparents had told them the Kingdom of Moshoeshoe stretched this far before some white person in England arbitrarily drew a line in the sand while they were sheltering at Thaba Bosiu.

"But I thought our King was friends with the Queen," Boitumelo used to ask her grandfather each time he told her this story, but he would just click his tongue, shake his head slowly and look out his hut at the horses prancing in the fields with the black mountains in the background.

She had met Thaba there and had known him from childhood. He was the best horse rider in their age group, but his dream was to go and work in Johannesburg and the first step would be Bloemfontein to raise enough money for the big move. She found it ridiculous that rich people had to drive somewhere to ride horses when in their village everyone owned one. She often asked aloud what it really meant to be rich, if you had to pay to ride someone else's horses. Thaba would shrug and ignore her.

"I am tired, I want to sleep early today."

Boitumelo hid her smile. "Why, was work tough today?" Saturdays were a busy day for him and the barber shop opened longer hours. This was something else she did not understand. These rich people drove to a place to get their hair washed and cut. In the village, you took turns to do each other's hair and who on earth gets their hair washed in a shop. Sies!

"No, I just want to get some sleep before those crazy praying people wake me too early."

Twinstreams was famous as the confluence of two streams. The Braamfontein Spruit was the longest stream in Johannesburg, starting off, as the name suggested, in Braamfontein and winding its way through various suburbs before meeting the Sand Spruit in Twinstreams and then together flowing into the Jukskei River near a huge prison. The horse-riding school had set up shop there because of the streams and the green belt, which combined to form a picturesque setting for the little suburb that the locals fondly called the *garden village of the north*. It had lush green vegetation, abundant bird life and a nature reserve next to a German sports club where you could enjoy a German beer and Eisbein, and watch people play tennis or five-a-side football.

Such was the tranquillity of the place that you wouldn't believe it if someone told you the N1 freeway was only a few hundred metres away, bordering the suburb. Well, you could not exactly call it a freeway because Thaba had told Boitumelo that rich people paid to drive on it. During the weekend and on some afternoons, she saw a lot of people riding bicycles along the streams and Thaba had told her that a lot of those bicycles cost more than R50 000 each. More urban nonsense she could not fathom. That was enough to buy a small RDP house! In Lesotho, she could go anywhere without paying to walk in the mountains or drive on the roads in her late father's old jalopy. Sure, you needed to push it downhill to start, but after that it was bliss when they had taken it out for a ride once a week, before they had left the village.

"Those church people are such a nuisance," hissed Thaba, breaking Boitumelo out of her reverie.

Directly opposite their little camp, across the stream, Marcus looked out from his bar and sighed heavily at the growing number of shacks in the area. He could see their fires as some of the squatters huddled against the cold. Some were cooking and the rising smoke danced in his security light like his own private version of a cheap aurora borealis.

"And to make matters worse, those church people will be waking us up early in the morning," he grumbled to his wife, while handing her a glass of Chateau Angelus 1996 from his favourite place in France, St Emilion. He had once spent two weeks in the village in Bordeaux, delighting in French gastronomy, playing *petanque* and croquet, hiking and drinking the best wines in the world. This had been in the summer of 1990, while a student in Poitiers, the city where Charles Martel halted the advance of the Saracens in 732.

Thandi took the wine from him, briefly took in its smell, and smiled. "Heaven!" she whispered as she perched on a bar stool.

The bar was a gift to him that she had secretly worked on while he was on one of those business trips from whence he routinely returned with local or international wines, depending on to where he had travelled. The smile on his face upon his return had been priceless when she had casually led him to the swimming pool area. The bar was in a thatched gazebo at an angle from the pool, facing the house but with a view to the stream in the east and yet taking in the sun's setting rays in the west. In the middle was his framed Zidane shirt from his first world cup in 1998. Next to it was a framed shirt of Steven Gerrard, from his beloved Liverpool team. She had then tastefully added pictures from some of their family holidays, a Bob Marley poster, a picture of the back of a solider with rifle and guitar on his back from the Vietnam war and more Liverpool memorabilia.

"Don't stress about them," she said.

"Yes, but apart from the fact that they are breaking by-laws with all this noise pollution, they shouldn't be congregating at all with COVID-19!"

"They don't know any better," his wife tried to soothe him. "Londi was telling me that a lot of people in the township don't believe it affects black people."

Londi was their maid, a most fascinating character who lived in Alexandra township near Sandton. The family was fond of Londi and she had been with them ever since the boys had been born. She was an incredible insight in to township life. Marcus and his family never went to Alex, except when taking visiting overseas friends to Bra Joe's for some braaied meat and to watch township life go by. Soweto was, of course, a preferred destination: two Nobel Prize winners and all.

"It's not just in the townships, Thandi," he responded. "I have very educated people in the office asking why it is not affecting black people and they ask in a way that wants confirmation that it doesn't." He sighed again. "They keep asking me why it is only happening in China and Europe. You will be surprised how many people don't read a book or even a serious article from the moment they leave college or university. I hope Cyril will at least announce a lockdown and then we will have peace from the church for some time."

She threw her head back and laughed out loud. "We are facing a pandemic and you are worried about people singing to their God!"

"Well, He can hear them just as well if they don't shout when they pray!" He grabbed the remote and changed the bar television channel from football to News at 8.

"Looks like the president will be late. I'll switch back when he comes on," he sighed as he switched off the TV altogether to focus on talking to his wife of twenty-seven years. At the same time, he glanced back to the stream and watched the moonlight shimmering on the water as if dozens of fireflies were dancing over the surface. He loved that time of day and switched on the Bluetooth speaker and played Enya's *Sun in the stream*.

They were immigrants from Zimbabwe and had lived in South Africa since 2008, the year he had had the final straw. He did not consider himself an economic refugee, although things had become tougher since they'd moved. The family had moved in 2008 when the supermarkets in that country had gone empty for weeks on end. Add to that the withdrawal of the main opposition party from the second round of the elections and he and his wife had decided they could not give away another five years of their lives to uncertainty. A promising country had been brought to ruin through decades of mismanagement but, despite that, they were doing well.

He had been a director in a large firm, living in a paid-up house and owning a second property, also paid up. He was working towards buying a second one so that his two sons would have the start that he never had. Life had been good until the opposition in Zimbabwe decided they had been beaten into submission. He had secured a job within weeks of the decision to relocate and had moved his family the same year, not just to continue a life of wine, food and culture but also to give his sons a more stable environment for them to pursue their dreams. The move had left its psychological scars, though.

Now, across the stream from his house, he was looking at immigrants from another country, Lesotho, trying to make it. Being a lefty, this was not a problem for him at all. The huge issue was that the crime rate had gone up as soon as the squatters had arrived. Add to that the littering of the river bank and the weekly praise and worship on Sunday mornings that would have rivalled a music festival and he was happy to back an operation to move them elsewhere. But the laws of South Africa, given its own very painful history, did not allow for that. So it was alarm beams, thicker and higher walls by his neighbours, electric fencing or barbed wire; a sight which shocked all his friends from France whenever they visited. Not a single visitor failed to register their shock at the high walls and electric fences as he drove them from the airport. He, of course, had to do with a palisade fence because of the view. Otherwise, why buy a house by the river?

A flurry of messages buzzed in from different WhatsApp groups and they both picked up their phones. The president was about to speak. He looked weary but determined and they both could tell, from the moment he said, "Fellow South Africans," that there would be a lockdown. Despite the stories coming out of China, Italy and Spain, no one had anticipated the extent of the lockdown. One thing was clear, WhatsApp groups and the Twitterati right across the country were full of praise for the president's leadership and his decisiveness in closing the country down for twenty-one days, starting in three days' time. Even the World Health Organisation chimed in with a message of congratulations.

I

Black Mountain

I and I build a cabin
I and I plant the corn
Didn't my people before me
Slave for this country?
Now you look me with that scorn
Then you eat up all my corn
We gonna chase those crazy
Chase them crazy
Chase those crazy baldheads out of town
Build your penitentiary
We build your schools
Brainwash education
To make us the fools
Hate is your reward for our love
Telling us of your God above

Bob Marley – Crazy Baldheads

The rains failed to come for the third year in a row. The village had never seen sheep show ribs before. Grazing was more than scarce, the sparse yellow grass having long disappeared, and the water in the mountains was tough for the livestock to reach. The horses were dying from the drought and a lack of grazing and were trying to reach streams on dangerous peaks. The granaries were nearly empty and families were rationing food. Malnutrition was not far away, as the children's increasingly distended bellies were beginning to show.

Thaba's father, who had borrowed money from the loan sharks in town two years ago, at the onset of the drought, could not bear it any longer. The threatening phone calls and SMSes did not stop. He woke up very early one morning and, without a word, strode out of the hut towards the mountains. He walked briskly in the dark, before the sun's rays kissed the horizon, his favourite blanket wrapped around his shoulders. He did not have his hat with him. A villager out tending his sheep and horses on the early morning dew greeted him and, when he did not receive a response, followed him from a distance, puzzled at where he was going without a hat. He was near enough to see, but too far away to stop him from flinging himself off the cliff. He was the third farmer to do so that year. The shepherd ran wildly back to the village, not minding the rocks, stumbling, falling and getting up, his voice hoarse, hoping for someone to respond.

In her hut, Thaba's mother stirred and heard the cries. Her blood froze when she reached out beside her in the dim of the hut to an empty floor mat. She heard someone shout her husband's name and she started wailing. Thaba dashed out of the hut where he slept with his younger brother. He saw the shepherd, wild eyed, running towards their village as other men poured out of their huts.

After an arduous two-hour effort, they retrieved Thaba's father's mangled body from the ravine and brought it back to the village. Thaba looked at his uncomprehending little brother and his mother, her body heaving with grief, between wailing and sobbing, and he decided there and then that he would not remain captive to the whims of the seasons. A month after the funeral, he sat down with his mother and announced his intention to go and look for work in South Africa.

"Mme, I need to raise money and send Bosiu to school. Otherwise he will be a farmer like father and we don't know what will happen in the future."

"Who will look after our horses, my son?" His mother had feared this moment would come. More and more young men were leaving their ways to go in search of a better life.

"Mme, we can leave them under Uncle's care. We do not have that many anyway. I will send you money for food every month. Look at Uncle; my cousin is sending money from the mine every month."

His mother shifted uncomfortably. It was too soon and she needed her son by her side. Johannesburg was so far away. She remembered when she once went there for a wedding with her husband. She did not like the way the women dressed and swung their hips when they danced. They were loud, brash and only interested in taking other men's money in her view. She wanted her son to marry a proper Sotho girl.

"Those mines are dangerous, my son. Look at all the young people who come back old before their time and die of this lung disease thing that kills miners before the ancestors are ready to call them back. I can't afford to lose your father and you too. You are now the head of this family."

It was emotional blackmail, they both knew. Thaba tried to soften the blow of the news of his plans.

"Mme, I have been talking to Boitumelo. She also wants to go and work in South Africa. She is happy to go with me and I think her mother will agree if you talk to her. And, Mme, we don't even want to go to Johannesburg. I have been told Bloemfontein is a big city and there are big farms there. It is near and we can come and go easily. We don't even need passports. I can come and see you at month end."

Her face brightened and she smiled for the first time in a month. Everyone in the village had known those two would end up together, although this would be way too soon. But, she reminded herself, she had got married when she was sixteen and Thaba was already twenty-three. He was a man and her neighbour needed a strong son-in-law. She was glad her son wanted to do things properly, instead of eloping like many young people had been doing in the last few years, only to come back with a child in tow without the blessing of the parents and ancestors.

Because of the recent funeral, they could not have a gathering. Instead, Thaba's mother spoke to his uncle who approached Boitumelo's mother and informed her that their son was looking for a lifelong companion and he thought Tumi, using the diminutive of her name for effect, would be an excellent choice. He extolled her virtues, saying how she had been a model of decorum and good behaviour ever since her own father had passed away years before and she had not given anyone in the village any reason to gossip about scandalous behaviour. He said that, even though Thaba was the best horse rider in the village, parents must let the young people go to the city and try their fortune.

"It is not as if they are really going to a foreign country. Everyone knows Bloemfontein is part and parcel of Lesotho. These borders were drawn up by strangers."

Boitumelo's uncle nodded in agreement but said it was too soon after Thaba's father had passed away for him to be entertaining thoughts of marriage, adding that he was too young and he needed to first look after his own recently-widowed mother before taking on the responsibility of looking after another family. Boitumelo's mother sat silently, listening to the conversation but communicating messages via body language: a frown here, the hint of a smile there.

Thaba's uncle cleared his throat and resumed his charge. "Today, my brothers, our sons are required to be different men from our time. Thaba and Tumi are both going to look for work. Their combined income will help both families in a more effective way. We do not know when the ancestors will bring the rains back. All this nasty politics in the capital city is not good for our country, our land and our people. The ancestors will be unhappy for a long time and it does not matter how much we slaughter here, the ancestors are upset with the leadership! It is not our children's fault and they deserve better!" He paused and wiped his brow, subtly scanning the room for the temperature. Boitumelo's mother gave her brother a darting sideways glance. The highway was opening. Thaba's uncle continued, "Are we going to hold our children hostage for what those rich people are doing to destroy our ways?"

In the kitchen, Boitumelo held her breath. She was dressed in a blue blanket and *shweshwe* dress, complete with matching doek and comfortable flat shoes. She had discussed the meeting with her mother and her mother knew what to pass on to her uncles in terms of expectations. They understood that these were two young people going out to seek their fortune and that they did not have any money. The promise lay in the future and her mother did not want to stand in her way.

Her uncle cleared his throat, smiled and said the magic words, "We are happy for our daughter to leave with Thaba. They are both good children and we know they will look after each other."

The very few women in the hut let out a cheer and broke into song as someone from both ends was dispatched to fetch the two young people from their respective withdrawn places. Thaba walked in a few seconds before Boitumelo and, as she shyly glided in, he beamed at his future wife and then turned to his mother. She wore a radiant smile. It was like her healing had fully begun.

II

The Sun In The Stream

I wanna love you, and treat you right
I wanna love you, every day and every night
We'll be together, with a roof right over our heads
We'll share the shelter, of my single bed
We'll share the same room
Is this love, is this love, is this love
Is this love that I'm feelin'?

BOB MARLEY – IS THIS LOVE

Thaba was awoken from his dreams and the face of his smiling mother by a loud voice beseeching the Lord for prosperity. It seemed as if he had just fallen sleep and the church people had already arrived! At the same time, Marcus across the stream reached angrily for his phone, snatched his gown from the bedroom settee and walked into the kitchen to avoid waking his wife up. As he popped a Ristretto Italiano capsule into the Nespresso machine, he looked through the window and could see people in flowing white robes, men with long goatees and women swaying back and forth in full cry. One of the congregation was in the middle of the stream, naked down to his underwear, and what looked like the high priest of Haifa was praying for him. They started belting out a hymn, arms raised to the heavens and swaying from side to side. Their faces were a picture of concentration and elation and their voices easily breached the double glazed windows he'd had installed against the winter chill from the streams.

Marcus glanced down at his speed dial numbers. He had five of them: his wife, his sons and the rest for armed response and city police. It rang a few times before a man who sounded like he had just been woken up answered.

"Police station, how can I help you?"

"Morning, I am calling from Twinstreams."

"Yeeees?"

"There are people making a hell of a din here!"

"A what?"

"A racket!"

"Sorry, I don't follow you. Can you speak clearly?"

"It is six o'clock on a Sunday morning and there are people making a noise, singing by our river!"

"You mean an African church?"

"I don't care what type of church it is. Can you come and remove them, please?"

"No, no, no, my brother. Those people are practising their religion. It is part of our culture!"

Marcus could not believe what he had just heard.

"What? They are breaking by-laws and there's a guy who is half-naked in the river. My wife can't even make tea without seeing naked people in the river every…"

"My brother, they are going to be there for an hour. Let them be! Let them pray! They are praying for you and the country."

"Listen, the president announced a national lockdown and…"

And the phone went dead before Marcus could accuse the policeman on the line of dereliction of duty. He immediately scrolled to his street enclosure WhatsApp group and began typing furiously, asking his neighbours whether they could hear the noise and asking the security representative to call the local security to come and move the congregants along. A few neighbours joined in to say they could hear the singing and what a disgrace it was, asking what use there was in having a councillor when she couldn't do her job and why were they were paying taxes if laws could not be respected and the police could not do their job? The security representative responded a minute later to say that the security company was sending a van but that they could only make a show of force and hope the church dispersed and could not touch them. The law governing security companies did not extend to Sunday-morning worshippers. One of his naughty neighbours suggested he place his speakers on the patio and play Michael Jackson's *Black or White* full blast.

Marcus sighed. He seemed to sigh a lot these days. He wondered to no one in particular why one would buy a house by a river for the country feel, only to be force-fed city sounds like a goose by people who travelled a long way to find flowing water by which to pray. "At least with a goose, you get *foie gras*! What is this by the rivers of

Babylon nonsense," he muttered to himself as he slouched back to the bedroom and closed the door firmly, in a vain attempt to shut out the Sunday world unfolding outside his palisade fence.

"Even the ducks have left for the day," he said to no one in particular as he crawled back in to bed, coffee cup forgotten in the kitchen. On cue, the hadedas, also upset at being awoken at this vile hour on a Sunday, began their cacophony, complaining that the humans in white robes were back. As they flew over Marcus' house, they seemed to cackle even louder, as if to say, "And what are you doing about it with your fancy bedroom slippers and gown?" They knew him by sight from his frequent excursions into the garden, where he either read a book or newspaper, or spoke on his phone..

The garden was a bird's paradise, with more than a dozen species competing for space for their nesting. The hadedas were the biggest of all the birds. Usually, hadeda and man tolerated each other at this point but, if ever any of them made a sound, he threw pebbles at them for disturbing his Sunday morning ritual. Hadedas were so loud that even Spanish national team player Xavi Alonso complained about them during the 2010 world cup. Still, Marcus had a soft spot for one of them. It seemed to have been injured somewhere and spent its time limping in the garden. He'd surprised his family by changing the wifi name to Limping Hadeda. The biggest creature in the garden, though, was a fairly plump rock dassie that had appeared out of nowhere and had taken up residence, somewhere between the wall and the Wendy house. Despite its beautiful plumage, he did not like the African Hoopoe that would perch on one of the side mirrors of his car and peck at its image in the window, occasionally setting off the car alarm. It also had a penchant for pooping on the car whenever it came from the car wash.

Thandi woke up an hour later and reached for the gown she had bought from Beijing Street on their last holiday in Guangzhou. It was a deep red silk gown with Chinese writing, a fire-breathing dragon on either side at the front and a full-body-size Chinese woman fanning herself at the back. She walked to the kitchen to make some tea. To call her a tea addict would be putting it mildly. She had a whole shelf dedicated to teas and a collection of differently styled tea pots. All her friends who travelled the world knew the best gift to bring her was a tea or tea pot from a different country.

She dialled Londi their maid's number.

Under South Africa's immigration rules, a family could bring their maid with them because South Africa was a big proponent of mother tongue instruction. A maid helped raise children while a family settled in a new country, but that is not the reason Marcus and Thandi had brought her with them. They strongly believed in hiring local people wherever they went because it was the right thing to do and also was a way of giving back to whichever country they were in. They and the children loved Londi, and they had moved her with them when Marcus had got a new job in Harare the capital city, four hundred kilometres away from where they had been living.

In 2008, the country had broken every single negative economic record there was to break. Supermarket shelves were as bare as dry bones, the ruling ZanuPF party was wreaking havoc across the land and they just could not leave her behind in that situation. There was an added important reason: she also happened to be from what was known as Fingoland, about thirty kilometres outside Bulawayo. Fingoland was the home of amaMfengu, a people from South Africa's Eastern Cape. In fact, they are a people who survived and fled the Mfecane wars and subsequently integrated into Xhosa, Thembu and Mpondo culture. They had proved their mettle in battle and it was Cecil John Rhodes who then brought them into Zimbabwe to try and counter the Matebele in war.

Marcus and Thandi had asked Londi whether she wanted to stay or not and, after consulting her mother, she decided to leave with Thandi and the children to South Africa as soon as the children finished the school year, three months after Marcus had left to start work. Londi settled happily in Johannesburg and lived in their home but, as she got used to the city, she'd wanted a little bit more independence and, in time, had gone to rent a room in Alexandra Park.

Marcus and Thandi loved to entertain with good company, quality conversation, food and wine. It was something they had always done from the time they'd got married. One Sunday lunch, about six months after their arrival in South Africa, Marcus had invited a friend he'd met on a UNDP building project in the Eastern Cape. The guy, Thembi, was a very friendly and hospitable quantity surveyor whose firm managed the project. Marcus always made it a point to work with local professionals. Thembi was genuinely curious about Zimbabwe, asking questions ranging from what went wrong with Robert Mugabe, was it really true that supermarket shelves were empty, how could a country with so much potential go wrong with such educated people… and so the questions carried on.

They'd shared many a glass of whisky together at his home in East London, but their friendship really took off when they discovered they were both Land Rover people and shared a common love for African music and history. They took to driving together to site, whenever Marcus was in town, just to talk about the different African songs, especially from Mali and Senegal. Being fluent in French, Marcus delighted in explaining the meaning of some of the lyrics to add to the richness of the musical heritage. Marcus would often say to Thembi, "One has to be *un homme de qualite*". It sounded better to say it in French.

During one of the dinners at their house, Marcus was asking about the whole fuss of clan names in the Eastern Cape and Thembi happened to mention, by way of example, that his wife was Mfengu and that is why he sometimes called her MaKhumalo.

"What?" exclaimed Marcus. "Our maid, Londi, is a Mfengu too!"

"Really? Didn't you say she came with you from Zimbabwe?"

"Indeed!" and turning to Bulelwa he added, "We have your people in our country. They are fully Zimbabwean of course, but they have maintained the Xhosa culture and language."

Then followed a long history lesson from both sides on how the Mfengus had come to be Xhosa, the different clan names in the Eastern Cape and, of course, how some of them ended up in Zimbabwe, having travelled there with Cecil John Rhodes.

"I have to meet this lady," declared Bulelwa and thus it was decided: the next time they were in Johannesburg on their way to some overseas holiday, they would spend a full day in Johannesburg, instead of a night at the airport hotel, and come for lunch.

Literally a month later, they were seated at lunch and neither Thembi nor Bulelwa could believe how fluent Londi was in Xhosa and that there was a whole group of people in Zimbabwe who not only spoke Xhosa fluently, but also practised all the rituals exactly the way they were practised in the Eastern Cape.

"You know, all this xenophobia nonsense and borders simply doesn't make sense," sighed Thembi.

"You know!" responded Marcus.

"Maybe we can help Londi trace the village or area where she comes from. We can start in Butterworth. If we ask her to speak to her grandmother…"

"You never know!" Thandi got excited by the idea adding, "I will ask her to phone tomorrow and by the time you guys get back from holiday, we will have as much information as possible to work with!"

III

Butterworth

Misty mornin', don't see no sun;
I know you're out there somewhere having fun.
There is one mystery – yea-ea-eah – I just can't express:
To give your more, to receive your less.
One of my good friend said, in a reggae riddim,
"Don't jump in the water, if you can't swim."
The power of philosophy –
yea-ea-eah – floats through my head
Light like a feather, heavy as lead;
Light like a feather, heavy as lead, yeah.

BOB MARLEY – MISTY MORNING

Londi picked up the phone, saw the missed call and called her employer Thandi back. She had left it on the charger and had gone to the Easter Monday service. Eleven years ago, she had met friends of her employers and, after a lunchtime conversation, had embarked on an incredible search for the home of her ancestors. Amazingly, she had not only found the area where her people came from before they'd left for Zimbabwe but also the village where she came from, just outside Butterworth. It had taken the best part of six months to trace back her origins, following several phone calls between her, her mother and grandmother back home in Bulawayo – with Thandi, listening on speaker phone, making copious notes and passing them on to Bulelwa. The two wives had become good friends and they had been determined to do as much as they could to succeed in this search, which had taken on more significance than a fun adventure.

As soon as the president announced there was going to be a lockdown for twenty-one days, Marcus and Thandi felt Londi would not be safe in Alexandra Park, what with the population density, and asked her to consider coming back to stay with them for the duration of the lockdown. Expressing her thanks for their thoughtfulness, she countered with an idea of her own suggesting that, since she was not going to be working anyway, she go instead to her cousins in Butterworth.

Her cousins did not live in the village but in Butterworth town itself. It was on the N2 highway from East London to Mthata, and the streets were always full of people. She had never, in her life, seen a small town with so many people in the streets. Given the high unemployment in the area, she wondered where they got the money to do the non-stop shopping that she saw every time she was there. It was not as if the social grant amount that government paid to its people was enough for a full month's shopping. No one could explain it to her.

There were a few government offices in the town, a magistrates' court, police station and teachers. And yet the town's shops and pavements were full of people. Even when people explained that husbands working in the mines sent money home every month, she could still not fathom the depth of spending that kept many shops, a lot of them with national branding, buzzing with business. Almost all the major national brands – from clothing through insurance to fast food – were located in the small town centre, which was really only one street. They competed against dozens of local stores, selling everything from hardware to fish and chips.

"Hello, Londi."

"Hello, Mama, how are you and the boys?" She never asked about Marcus. It was just that way.

"We are all fine, keeping safe. How are you doing?"

Londi hesitated and wondered whether to tell her employer that she had been to church. She had been given a lecture about social distancing and hand washing but especially on the dangerous belief that Covid-19 did not affect black people. When the news was on in the house, they showed her, on six different news channels, that this thing was all over the world and affecting people of every race and social background. But, when she'd got to Butterworth, her cousins had reminded her that the local pastor was a great man of God and pointed out that this thing only affected rich people, like tourists and her boss, who travelled on aeroplanes all over the world.

"Look at the people here. Do you see anyone dying, like in that Italy you keep mentioning?" her cousins would ask mockingly. They loved her and loved to show her off as their cousin from Zimbabwe, but sometimes they felt she sounded too much like those people from the big city, what with her superior knowledge. She didn't want to prolong that impression and, rather than present the facts to them, preferred to keep the peace and have a good time peacefully.

Before long, she was persuaded to drop her guard and was out in the streets with everyone else. The police came and beat up a few people but they could not come back every day. Many of them were on duty on the highway and regional roads anyway, looking for people who were rumoured to be trying to get back from the Western Cape for Easter or funerals. The people could not miss the funerals of their families. What would the ancestors say?

The pastor asked the congregation to come in, one and all but, curiously, the front row seemed to have been moved further back from the pulpit than normally was the case. The pastor immediately launched into fire and brimstone mode. God was judging the nations, he declared. The world had never come to a standstill before, even during two world wars when all countries were fighting. "That is why it was called a world war!" he thundered. Not all the weapons in the world could stop divine punishment and it was the super powers of Europe and America that were facing God's wrath first, because they had lost their way with sin and iniquity, a modern Sodom and Gomorrah!

The choir, three of whom carried his children, were leading the Amen replies as he strutted back and forth in his all-white attire, from shoes to suit to tie. This was the time for all believers to sow their trust in God and the only way to sow was to pay their tithes like never before. He declared that God saw every giving heart and would replenish their granaries tenfold, if only they had true faith. When he talked about tithes, the choir hummed a stirring slow tune, arms clasped together in front. After the anointed plates had gone and returned full of coins and notes, the pastor gave a shorter sermon. The Amens rang out again and the choir soon stood and led the church in a rousing rendition of *How Great Thou Art*.

Londi walked back to her cousins' small house. Butterworth was not its usual filthy self. Normally, it was a mess of litter all over the streets, loud music blaring at a street corner from a gospel musician selling CDs and small shops competing for the same attention with their shop-front speakers blaring music directly onto the pavement. The traffic was absent. On Fridays, it could take half an hour just to drive through Butterworth central, as people drove from Mthata to East London for the weekend through the virtually one-street town. Usually, the town was a riot of colour as the grandmothers queued for social grants, the young unemployed men hung around every side street corner leading to the townships and villages and young girls vied for their attention.

She turned left at Heavenly Fish and Chips, a shop that always had queues going round the corner for the popular greasy chips and Russian sausages. It was shuttered closed, like most of the shops in the town. The liquor store next door to it had been boarded up with wood after some unknown people had broken the glass during the night and made off with thousands of Rands-worth of liquor. Everyone knew who had done it, but no one had seen anything because they were all buying from the gang, since alcohol sales had been banned. She walked into the house behind her cousins and made straight for the phone on the charger.

"I am fine, thank you, Mama. Butterworth is quiet but in the township people are mixing in the streets and children are playing outside.

"Oh, dear," said Thandi on the other side of the line.

"The houses are too small for them to stay inside all day. It drives them crazy," Londi offered by way of explanation.

"Yes, I understand," replied Thandi.

She had seen the television news reports of some of the townships and informal settlements. It was every middle-class person's nightmare. The idea of the pandemic catching fire in the super-crowded residential areas and engulfing their gentrified suburbs scared her. She had seen the reports about how the scourge was disproportionately attacking African Americans because of their vulnerability as a society at the coal face of the service industry, but also because they had more underlying illnesses. This made her think of what would happen in South Africa with its high number of cases of TB, diabetes and HIV and AIDS, as well as the widespread obesity in the nation. "It was too ghastly to contemplate," she thought, using one of her brother-in-law's favourite expressions since the outbreak was declared a pandemic by the World Health Organisation.

"But are you looking after yourself?" She forced her thoughts back to the call.

"Yes, Mama…"

"Who is that?" Thandi heard laughter in the background

"It is my cousins. They are making lunch."

"But…"

Londi quickly cut Thandi off.

"There's no water in the village. I thought it would be safer for hand washing to stay here where there's municipal tap water. They say the drought has been very bad."

"Oh, okay. Well, take good care of yourself. I will call you soon. Let us know if you need anything."

"I am fine for now, thank you, Mama." Londi put the phone down relieved and happy. Her employers cared for her and had paid her in full but had also given her extra, saying they knew people would take advantage of the situation and hike prices. They had also paid for the bus trip to East London on Greyhound and extra money for the taxi to Butterworth. She considered herself truly lucky and did not want to disappoint them, but there was no way she was going to be stuck for three weeks in a village. She replied to some WhatsApp messages from her mother back home in Bulawayo before putting the phone away. Despite being in the home of her ancestors, she could not bring herself to stop referring to Bulawayo as home.

In Twinstreams, the kettle started whistling and Thandi made herself a Chinese tea in a little heat-resistant glass teapot that comes ready made with infuser. It was an interesting way to make tea. You put the tea leaves in a little infuser, poured in the water and magic! She walked to the patio, feeling the warm rays of the rising sun. She looked out into the garden where she and Marcus had hosted many a party and Sunday lunch. The property sat on 1 500 square metres with a deck, swimming pool and the gazebo for the bar. The garden allowed her to indulge one of her other passions, gardening.

Having got rid of the imported varieties because they consumed a lot of water, there were lots of indigenous trees in the garden. On the left side of the garden, behind a rock formation and two huge Makalani Palm trees, she managed a vegetable and herb garden, where she grew pumpkin, sweet potatoes and tomatoes. The herb garden featured rosemary, thyme, parsley, rocket, coriander and chives. Since the declaration of the lockdown, Marcus had boldly announced his intention to take up gardening too and they'd planted carrots, lettuce, Swiss chard, onions and kale together. They'd also moved around a couple of aloes that had grown too big, so that friends of the children would not scratch themselves. She watched a Southern Masked Weaver set off on an early-morning raid for some unlucky worm. Hardly a minute later, it was back at its nest, worm in mouth, giving one quick, furtive glance around before disappearing into its upside down entrance. The circle of life.

Marcus walked out onto the patio in t-shirt, shorts and slippers. He had his car keys in his hand and announced he was going to the shops to get the paper. Despite watching news on television, reading papers online and following several news outfits on twitter, he still stuck to the tradition of buying the Sunday papers. He never bought newspapers during the week but somehow Sunday lent itself to lying back in the garden under the gazebo, with a glass of orange juice or a coffee, turning page after page, folding each section neatly by his side before reaching for the next. He asked Thandi whether she wanted anything from the shops. They had refused to panic buy because they did not wish to be part of the problem. It was their world view and attitude to life to always look for solutions to societal issues. As he eased his new Land Rover Defender out of the garage, he saw a young man walking on the other side of the communal electric fence.

Thaba crossed the stream gingerly and walked to work through the green belt, skirting the boomed off area of eleven houses that were protected by an electric fence. As he walked, a rock dassie darted from the river, through the electric fence and disappeared into the drain near one of the houses. Thaba saw a garage door gliding up and one of the home owners reversing his car out of the garage and wondered how much money one needed to live in a house that big and to own two cars. He had seen the man's wife driving an SUV.

At their little squatter camp, around their fires at night, the dwellers often spoke of the houses across the stream. They knew all of the owners by sight, knew which cars they and their wives drove, and sometimes marvelled at the fact that children in their teens also drove cars. Some houses had four or five cars parked in the driveway. There were black, white and Indian families on the same road, something he had not thought he would find in Johannesburg. He had heard it was a racist place and the suburbs were only for the whites. As he walked past the boomed off area and past the other houses along the green belt, dogs barked at him from each house he passed. His friend, who worked part time in the garden at the local vet, said the residents spent thousands of Rand just buying medicine for their pets, but he didn't believe him. Who would spend so much money on an animal?

"I am telling you! I spoke to Nomvula, and she told me that every visit is about R500 and some people go the vet three or four times a month," the guy would say. Nomvula was the receptionist and the guy had a huge crush on her.

"She is out of your league," Thaba would tell him. "How do we know she even talks to you? She probably does not even look at you."

"Chief, I have a degree in Chemistry. Don't look down on me because I can't find a job yet. If it was not for this permit thing, I would be living in one of those houses over there with Nomvula by my side and you would be working in my garden."

Thaba would burst out laughing and retort, "You Zimbabweans and your education. How do you come up with those funny names you give yourselves and why do you like English names?"

They would laugh before parting. His friend lived in another squatter camp near the highway with a group of waste pickers. They had met while waiting for piece jobs at a warehouse and stayed in touch, visiting each other on weekends to break the boredom of their misery. It was illusory, but it provided some relief.

His thoughts were interrupted by four cyclists on mountain bikes. He smiled to himself as he remembered another exaggeration from his learned neighbour, who claimed that people paid as much as R50 000 for a bicycle. That had not stopped him telling his wife the same thing! He left the green belt and joined the tarmac, heading to the local shopping centre where he worked. It had recently been upgraded and the barber shop was very busy at weekends and after hours. He walked into the barber shop and the look on the owner's face told him there was bad news coming.

"Morning, Thaba, how are you?"

"Morning, boss. I am fine, thanks, how are you?"

"Did you hear the news about the lockdown?"

"No, boss…"

"The president announced that the country is locking down for twenty-one days, in three days' time. In this shopping centre, only two places will remain open. The rest of us have to close because we are not essential services."

Thaba's heart started pounding so wildly he thought his boss could hear it.

"We are a very small business and I can't afford to pay you for those days."

Thaba sank to his chair and put his head in his hands.

His employer reached behind the counter and produced a shopping bag from the local supermarket.

"I bought some food to help you through the period. You can take it home after work."

Thaba took the bag and had a peek. There was a one kilogram packet of rice, a whole fresh chicken, which they put into the little drinks fridge in the shop, and some tinned food. His employer had helpfully put in some sweets and biscuits for Thaba's son. Thaba thanked him profusely and asked to be excused for a moment.

He walked briskly to the shopping centre toilet and wept silently and bitterly. He had lied that he lived in Cosmo City, renting a back room, when he'd first got the job. He didn't have a fridge! The chicken would have be to be cooked and consumed quickly. A whole chicken like that should last them a whole week. His mind was racing. Although he did not pay rent or have any other bills, he still needed to send money to his mother, something he had been doing monthly ever since he'd left the village. He was grateful for the food, but the shock of the announcement and the uncertainty of the future troubled him. He dried his eyes and left the toilet to go back to the barber shop.

As he walked out, he saw the man who drove a Land Rover emerge from the supermarket pushing a trolley. A quick glance showed a bouquet of flowers, a few bottles of wine and various food stuffs. It looked like he had a lot of rice too. The man walked into the liquor store and emerged almost immediately as Thaba walked back to the shop. There were no customers yet and the floor was still clean from yesterday, so Thaba hung around outside. The Land Rover man must have been put off by the queue in the liquor store. He walked past the barber shop with his trolley full of groceries. Thaba felt a wave of bitterness well up and course throughout his body at the unfairness of life. He watched the Land Rover man right until he turned towards the parking lot. Thaba walked into the barber shop and sat down, waiting for the first customers to arrive. One thought kept repeating itself in his head: how much rice did one family need?

Marcus allowed the burly Congolese car guard to unpack the trolley contents into the boot. He did it to give the guard some cash. Normally, he gave R5 at a time, something his wife criticised him for, saying the amount was too small. Someone in his football fan club had suggested they look out more for car guards as they were going to be hit hard by the absence of shoppers from stores. He stopped him from unpacking the ten packets of rice from the trolley, gave him R10, locked the car and pushed the trolley towards the pub where he watched literally all his football matches.

He asked for the owner, a very friendly but no-nonsense lady and, when she came out of her office near the kitchen, he told her the rice was a small contribution for the waiters, because he knew they would be hit hard by the lockdown. The government had decided to ban all alcohol sales, which meant the pub would be closed for three weeks. Almost all waiters in the country did not have salaries and lived off tips. How they managed to survive he didn't really know and had never asked. This time was different, though. He knew they would have absolutely no income. He handed over the bags, which were gratefully received, and the owner told him they were very concerned about their staff and had begun to put together some food parcels. His contribution would go a long way in helping. He left the pub, walked back to his car and drove home.

IV

Prohibition

She love to party, have a good time
She looks so hearty, feeling fine
She loves to smoke, sometime shiftin' coke
She'll be laughin' when there ain't no joke
A pimper's paradise, that's all she was now
A pimper's paradise, that's all she was
A pimper's paradise, that's all she was now
Pimper's paradise, that's all she was
Every need got an ego to feed
Every need got an ego to feed

Bob Marley – Pimper's Paradise

Mlibo and his friends were shocked. The government has just ordered all schools, colleges and universities shut. All students were required to leave their residences within seventy-two hours. He was a final year student at the school of medicine but, even though he did not live on campus, he also worked part time as a barman in the students' pub. He did it for fun and enjoyed Friday nights when the West African students from humanities would bring out their Koras and guitars and do a sing-along of rich African music. Sometimes, they threw in some Paul Simon compositions and played them African style.

Tonight was different, though, because everyone had been expecting an announcement and was watching from the common room. As soon as the president had finished addressing the nation, the pub had swelled in numbers and within a couple of hours had sold out all its stock. He saw opportunity. The next morning, he got into his Jeep Wrangler and headed straight to the bank at Campus Square. When the teller saw the amount of money he had written on the withdrawal slip, she became chatty. She looked beautiful in her bank uniform and neatly coiffed hair. She was well-spoken, too. He asked where she lived and she said Berea.

He was about to bring a swift conclusion to the chatting when, on second thoughts, he asked for her number. His girlfriend was leaving res and flying back home to Cape Town with other students from OR Tambo airport later in the day. Berea was too far from Fourways, where he lived alone in an apartment, but perhaps he could persuade the bank teller to stay with him during the lockdown. She swiftly wrote her number on the cash slip and stamped it in almost one movement. Somehow, he thought she had done this before when he saw the way she positioned her body away from the cameras behind the tellers. She could not take calls during hours and he promised to call as soon as the bank closed. Her eyes immediately sparkled.

Mlibo left the bank and walked back to his car, watching carefully that no one was following him. His father, also a medical doctor from the Midlands in KwaZulu-Natal, had a flourishing practice and was also doctor on call for the expensive private schools in the area catering for the children of the uber rich of South Africa. His son had gone to school at one of the schools as a day boarder. He had a large property portfolio in Cape Town, Durban and Johannesburg and had given his son the use of an apartment in an exclusive estate for the duration of his medical studies. On top of that, he had bought him the Jeep Wrangler as soon as he had passed his matric.

Now fully liquid with all the cash he had, Mlibo drove to a bottle store in the informal settlement near campus. Beers were much cheaper there and he was not worried about security because the people knew him there. Not only had he patched up many an injured gang leader in the hospital, he was also part of the medical team in white coats and luminous vests that performed sweeping visits of informal settlements at vaccination time. As he drove through the narrow streets, he chuckled to himself at the names of the spaza shops and beauty salons. There was *White House Spaza Shop*, nicely painted with the colours of a leading mobile phone operator. Further down was *Try My Best Spaza Shop*, painted in the bright colours of a rival mobile operator.

The beauty salons and barber shops were housed in large but narrow shipping containers featuring drawings that were clearly recognisable as Rihanna, Oprah and Beyonce. The barber shops had Usher, Jay Z and Drake. "Where are the local celebrities?" Mlibo mused to himself. The narrow streets were already full of people with many women, still in their night gowns, cigarettes dangling from their lips and child on their hips, walking to the small shops. There were carpenter shops and hardware shops run by Asians, who stood at the entrance to their shops and stared as he drove past. At a street corner, a man was selling sheep heads next to a fruit and vegetable market called the poor man's market. In the distance, at the end of the informal settlement, was a huge shopping mall.

A lot of the small shops were struggling to compete against the chain stores that were found in the malls. They could only compete on convenience because the malls opened late and closed early due to security fears. The armed response companies refused adamantly to let their drivers venture in to the informal settlements. Some of the shops were run from a hole in the wall from inside someone's small yard and this space was usually rented to Somalis and Pakistanis, people who were battle-hardened in trade negotiations, although the Somalis also had a unique and strong clan system. They bought product together and, therefore, got better discounts than the local owners of spaza shops.

Having trekked all the way from their country, fleeing the civil war and what was essentially a failed state, the Somalis also seemed to have a strong system of integrating newly-arrived Somalis who, after a period of apprenticeship in a Somali-owned shop, soon opened their own shop in another street. This led to tensions that were ruthlessly exploited by some rascals of politicians in times of crisis. Like in many countries in Europe, the accusing finger of prejudice was pointed at the stranger, the foreigner, the other, when a child went missing, was raped or simply because elections were coming up. Then the hospital would be really busy with traumatised victims bludgeoned, sometimes burnt, by angry mobs, with the police sometimes turning a blind eye. And yet, when there was no controversy, everyone got on well.

Mlibo parked outside one of the bigger houses and a thin, stern-looking lady came out. Her face broke in to a wide grin as she saw the young medical student who sometimes came with his friends to get stoked at her place. He usually brought foreign students with him, but this time he was alone.

"*Hey wena*, Mlibo!" she greeted him. "You are a bit early today." She never spoke quietly.

"I have not come to drink, Mama," he replied and then quickly added, "You know there's a lockdown coming in three days?"

"Yes, we heard Cyril was going to address us and we watched the news." She felt quite important as she said that.

"Well, do you know you won't be allowed to sell alcohol?"

"*Hey, wena?* I thought this man was with team white monopoly capital? What is this nonsense?"

"No, Mama. It is to make sure the lockdown works properly. The government must stop this novel…new coronavirus from spreading and, when people get together to drink, it is a major problem."

"*Hau, yebo?*"

"Yes, Mama."

"But this thing does not affect black people. It is only people who fly into the country, these white tourists! Why do they want to stop us drinking in the township? Are they going to close those fancy hotels where the disease comes from?"

"Everything is shutting down, Mama, except supermarkets, pharmacies and the like. It is called essential services."

"*Hey wena*, do you know how essential I am to this township? Our people come here to forget their problems. Now, if they lose their jobs, I am going to be even more essential! So why are you here then?"

"I want to buy some booze. Lots of it."

"Now you are talking," she guffawed. She clapped her hands vigorously, gave him a hug and planted a kiss on both his cheeks when he announced how much he wanted to buy and promptly declared him her best customer ever. He told her she must head to the bank straight away and put the money in the bank. It was better to have empty beer fridges but cash in the bank because no one knew how long the lockdown would really be. There was a possibility of extension he said, telling her about Italy and Spain. "And you don't have to worry about disappointing your local customers because you will be closed. And when they allow you to reopen, you can order fresh stock, Mama."

He bought fifty cases of twenty-four-pack beers in cans and some of the cheaper whiskeys and brandies and headed to his apartment in a small, stylish estate. He drove straight into his garage before looking for the estate gardener, a Malawian called Dickswell, who helped him unload his purchase into the space next to the Jeep. There was parking for two cars. Despite it being a two-bedroomed apartment, he preferred to stay alone and his father was quite strict on that score.

"You have to preserve property value," his father never ceased to tell him.

He paid the gardener a tip of R50 and wished him the best for the lockdown.

"Don't drink too much, Doctor," Dickswell said, laughing.

"Don't worry, Dickswell. I have some friends coming to stay with me. The university is closed and they can't go home to their parents."

"Okay, Doc. Thank you and see you in three weeks!"

Mlibo waved and got back into the car. He liked Dickswell, who did work for the gardens and public spaces for all twelve apartments in the small, upmarket residence. From time to time, Mlibo would pay him to come in on a weekend and give him leftover food from the braais he would host at the clubhouse for his girlfriend and a few other students. In return, Dickswell would clean up after the braai, grateful for the extra income.

Next, he drove to the hospital where they did their practical work, to show they had mastered the theory from the lecture hall, and declared himself available for duty, should he be needed. He explained that he was not going home like the other students but was staying at his apartment. His name was added to the list of medical personnel who would get a "Doctor's car" sticker.

The day before the lockdown began, he received a call to collect his sticker. It had his name and ID number and he stuck it on the windscreen, next to his licence disc, as instructed. Now, if any policeman stopped him, all he would need to do is point to the sticker and the policeman could scan it and confirm that he was indeed essential service personnel. He drove to a place where he knew he could buy an unregistered sim card off the streets, and drove back to his apartment, pulled out the mobile phone he'd used before the latest upgrade, and sent a message to a few of his trusted friends using the new number.

I have lots of booze, all sorts, will deliver. Please share this number only and give my name as Umlilo.

Later that afternoon, he drove back to campus and picked up his girlfriend and two other girls who had asked for a lift to the airport. He dropped them off at OR Tambo on time and hung around with his girlfriend until ten minutes before boarding. Since SAA had cut back on its domestic and international flights, the airport was not busy at all and there was no queue at the security check. She had already checked in online. The other girls had gone in ahead of his girlfriend.

"Babe, I won't see you for three weeks," he moaned softly. "You can board at the last minute. Let me sit here with you for a while."

"Oh sweet! How cute!" chorused her envious friends as they went to clear security. "Thank you, Mlibo, see you on the other side of lockdown!" The two carefree students bounced through the security check and left him with his girlfriend.

In reality, he wanted to kill time so that he could head to Berea straight from the airport and avoid two round trips. He talked softly with her, reminding her to remember to study because, with lectures cut short, there would be a lot of catching up to do. Finally, he kissed his girlfriend goodbye and, as soon as she disappeared from sight, whipped out his phone. The banks were closed by now.

"Hello…" The voice on the line was hesitant.

"Hi, it's me. We met this morning at the bank?"

"Oh, hi!" The voice tone changed immediately from amber to green.

"So, have you finished work?"

"Yes, I am on my way to the taxis."

"I have a suggestion to make," he said tentatively.

"Yes?"

"First, do you live with your family…" he probed

"No, I share a place with a friend from church."

"Sorry, what is your name by the way?"

"Babalwa…"

"I am…." He began

"Mlibo, I know," she interrupted before quickly adding, "I saw it on the withdrawal slip".

He couldn't believe it. This was too easy. He made his suggestion as he drove out of the parkade and entered her address on his GPS. She was coming to spend the lockdown with him and he was going to pick up her up because the taxi would get her home before he got there. He was a bit nervous. He knew the township near campus quite well but was nervous about Berea being close to Hillbrow. His GPS was going to take him right through the notorious area.

He lowered the volume of the music in his car for full alertness, his ears straining for any unusual noise and his eyes avoiding direct contact with any other driver when he stopped at a traffic light. It unnerved him when a car stopped next to him and the occupants stared. He had heard too many stories of crime in Hillbrow and he avoided it at all costs.

He made it to Berea safely, though, and parked at the side of a large apartment block. There must have been over a hundred apartments in that building. Some of them had loud music blaring from balconies while others had washing lines competing with braai stands. He put his phone on speaker and dialled Babalwa's number. He did not want to put it to his ear in case of a smash and grab. Babalwa came bouncing out of her apartment with her roommate in tow, who immediately locked eyes with him. He looked around nervously and unlocked the door. Her friend opened the back door and thrust Babalwa's bag onto the floor of the Jeep. Babalwa introduced her friend who was wearing a cropped t-shirt that exposed her midriff. She had melons for breasts and Mlibo quickly pushed aside the crazy thought of inviting them both. Babalwa was beautiful in her own right and looked even more dazzling out of her bank uniform. He didn't want to hang around, quickly greeted the friend and made up some excuse for wanting to leave right away.

The friend laughed loudly and teased him. "Why are you in a hurry Mister! You have twenty-one days!"

The two girls laughed while Mlibo grinned like an idiot. "I just want to get to the shops on time. People are panic buying and there are queues…" he offered.

"No worries," the friend replied and winked at him. Her smile said it all. She was available too, if he dared call her secretly. "Take good care of my friend, neh?"

"Of course," he replied. "That won't be an issue at all."

He eased into the road, made a u-turn and headed back to the main road that would take him to the Joe Slovo on ramp and the safety of the M1. Babalwa laughed when she noticed how nervous he was.

"Relax!" she said smiling, "You are safe here. People drive to Ellis Park for soccer and rugby all the time and they use this road. Some white people park their cars on the street here and walk to the stadium. It is only dangerous when you go deep into Berea or Yeoville and then only if you act like a visitor. He laughed out loud, feeling foolish. His privilege was showing, as his friends used to say to him on campus whenever he uttered some suburban "absurdity", like walking the family dogs back home in the Midlands. His friends would tease him and say, "Walking the dogs in the countryside? You mean hunting! Oh, by the way, you people buy food for your dogs, and then you take them for exercise!"

He had given up explaining that they lived in a country estate with strict rules about pets without a leash because that just made it worse. He on ramped and sped up a bit. The sudden surge of the Jeep and the pressure of the car seat at her back made Babalwa giddy.

"Do you mind if I take a selfie?" She giggled gaily like a school girl. It was going to be a great three weeks.

"I will send my location as soon as I get there," she had promised her roommate in response to her concern about the rate of femicide in the country, after the initial excitement at the news had died down. "I looked at his Facebook account after he left and then I googled him. He seems to come from a good family and his social media pages are all about medicine and studies. He is going to be a doctor. I think I am safe with him." She'd paused before saying, "And my boyfriend won't find out because he will be in lockdown!"

They'd roared with laughter at their complicity. A doctor certainly offered a more promising future than her boyfriend, who kept changing jobs and blaming foreigners for taking them. Besides, he had struck her on two occasions when she had tried to convince him to persevere in at least one job. She had had to miss work without explanation on both days because of a black eye. She didn't know why she forgave him each time he apologised.

The Jeep swept towards Fourways after off ramping at William Nicol. She didn't really know this part of town well, though she remembered a childhood trip to Montecasino, when their entire family had visited their big city cousins one Christmas ages ago, soon after the dawn of democracy. Everyone had wanted to see this Johannesburg where all the men went to work in the mines. Pity she couldn't ask to be taken for dinner there because of the lockdown. He turned off William Nicol and drove towards Estate Tranquil.

"Wow!" she thought to herself as she tried to maintain her composure as he slowed before a massive gate flanked by a high wall topped by an electric fence. He pressed one of the buttons on his remote control and the gates glided open and closed behind her. He pressed a second button and a second gate opened. Two whole gates! The units were spaced apart and she saw some of the most beautifully manicured lawns and gardens she had ever seen in her life. He cruised slowly past four units before turning into a short driveway. He pressed another button on the remote and the garage door rose and disappeared into the garage ceiling. She felt like she was in a Hollywood movie! The garage was almost as big as her apartment.

She had gone to school in her village in Lusiksiki in the Eastern Cape, studied at Walter Sisulu University in Mthata and the first time she had come to Johannesburg as an adult was when she got the job at the bank. To date, her daily commute had been from Berea, down Empire Road and straight to Campus Square, where the branch was located. On weekends, she stayed in the flat watching soapies with her friend or her boyfriend would pick them up in his friend's car and they would go to a braai in Thembisa or eat fish with the Congolese down the street in Yeoville.

She stepped out of the Jeep and noticed the beers and other drinks on the garage floor and gasped! This was more drinks than her boyfriend could buy her in one year!

"Are these all your drinks?" she exclaimed.

"No, no…" he laughed. "My friends have been kicked out of res and they don't have space in their homes. So we bought drinks and I can drop them off on my way to the hospital. I will be on duty from time to time for this virus thing."

He shut the garage, took her bag out of the back of the car and opened the door into the kitchen. She had only ever seen kitchens like this in magazines or television. Everything was built in; there were shiny buttons and dark wood everywhere. She stood there nervously for a second and he motioned her to follow him into the lounge, where he casually dropped her bag next to a leather sofa. It occurred to her that the giant curved smart TV in front of her was the same brand as everything in the kitchen, as if someone had gone to one shop to buy everything on one day. She sank in to the couch, a little bit flustered, and Mlibo smiled to himself.

"You want something to drink?"

"Yes, please. Do you have any ciders?"

"Of course. Coming right up!"

He walked back to the kitchen and returned with a cider and a beer, kicked off his shoes and sat next to her on the couch, leaning back sideways against the arm so he could face her.

"Cheers," he said and, smiling, added, "So… Tell me about yourself."

V

Bile

No sun will shine in my day today
(No sun will shine)
The high yellow moon won't come out to play
(Won't come out to play)
Darkness has covered my light
(And the stage) and the stage my day into night
Now, where is this love to be found?
Won't someone tell me 'cause life (sweet life)
Must be somewhere (sweet life) to be
found (somewhere, somewhere for me)
Instead of a concrete jungle
Where the living is hardest (in a concrete)

BOB MARLEY – CONCRETE JUNGLE

Nature seemed to sense the mood in South Africa as the skies darkened the morning after the announcement. Grey clouds turned into dark clouds by late afternoon, but there was none of the rolling thunder that is so typical of Johannesburg storms. Instead, it started drizzling silently that night.

Boitumelo woke up to a steady drip drip sensation on her forehead. She touched her face and it was wet. It was raining and the shack was leaking! She shook Thaba to wake him up. Normally a very responsible parent and husband, he had unusually drunk himself into a stupor and had staggered back to the shack and fallen asleep within seconds. She shook him harder and, as he emerged from the fog of deep sleep, the rain intensified. A heavy, silent drizzle, gaining in strength and trickling into the shack made from plastic and cardboard. The flimsy cover to their one room shack flapped gently in the wind.

The rain started trickling to the ground and seeping into the shack. It was part pitter-patter on the plastic sheets and part steady dull drone on the cardboard, but it was relentless. Their son stirred and started crying. Boitumelo reached for him and tried to keep him dry and warm from the icy chill that was infiltrating itself into their bodies. Thaba went to try and fix the entrance to the shack and for a brief moment, the super moon burst through the clouds and he caught a glimpse of his wife's face when he stretched his hand out for a string. It was glistening and he knew it was not rain pouring down from her eyes. He placed a stone at the bottom to try and hold the plastic sheets together and used the string to fashion a tight knot at the top. It worked. Temporarily. He moved back into the one corner where the rain was not too bad and held his wife and child. Nobody made a sound and they sat for two hours in that position, grim faced, with clenched teeth, summoning whatever little dignity they had left in bitter silence. The rain did not ease up but they fell asleep because of the sheer despair of it all, too tired to care. It was cold, miserable and wet for the rest of the night.

The roar of the stream woke them up. The rain had subsided and Thaba stepped out of the shack onto muddy ground. The stream was swollen, frothing, angry, swirling where the two streams clashed before storming downstream at a furious pace. Other shack dwellers were emerging from their shacks, unable to look each other in the eye, defeated and humiliated by the twin forces of nature and poverty.

Thaba and a couple of other men jogged away from the green belt and stables, past a small shopping centre and across Rivonia Road to the local giant hardware store, which normally discarded cardboard and plastic into a municipal skip. They sold bulk items and often had discarded material that was useful for shack building. Thaba hoped the dustbin men had not been round. He envied them. They were considered an essential service and did not have to stop working.

They lifted the lid of the skip and were greeted by more despair. The skip was empty. The hardware must have made special arrangements to clean up immediately after the lockdown. Even the rats, which were not scurrying away at the sight of the homeless, looked disappointed as they looked for non-existent food. With restaurants and fast food outlets closed, it was already proving to be tough for the rats. For a moment, rodent and shack dweller were united in grief and anxiety. Thaba trudged back to the camp, cursing the day he had left Lesotho, angry with his father for committing suicide and at God for the drought that had triggered the suicide in the first place.

He entered the shack and was greeted by the red, weeping eyes of his wife, cradling their baby.

"What's wrong," he asked, almost absurdly.

"Most of the food has been damaged," she sniffed, pointing to the corner of the shack where they had fashioned a log into a table. After falling sleep, they must have knocked it over. All the dry biscuits Thaba's employer had bought were destroyed. Some of the tinned foods were covered with mud. He retrieved them and without a word went to wash them by the banks of the stream. He had to be careful not to fall in.

As he leaned back, he picked up movement in the Land Rover house directly in front of him as the lady of the house walked into her kitchen. The soft warm glow of the lights in her house taunted him and, as the drizzle started again, he felt the bile rise in him.

It did not stop raining for three days, during which time the stream rose higher and higher and they huddled closer and closer in their soggy prison, their child's crying at times driving him insane and at others bringing them both to tears. This was wrong and unfair and Thaba's hot shame was turning into a deep, seething anger, eating away at the core of his values and everything he stood for.

He remembered the Land Rover man's trolley and, on the fourth day after wrestling with his conscience all night, awoke at three in the morning, with a steely determination in his eyes glinting like a fading star. He was careful not to awaken his wife and quietly made his way out of the shack. He took the blunt knife that he'd laboured with to open the now finished tinned fish and made his way towards the place where he usually crossed the stream on his way to work. The rain had stopped in the late afternoon of the third day and the stream had somewhat subsided.

He had to be careful; the rocks that he used as stepping stones were treacherously wet and slippery. He slipped and grazed his shin and knee on one of them and screamed silently, the pain shooting through his entire leg. He closed his eyes in a vain attempt to stop the pain, teeth clenched for what seemed like an eternity. Composing himself, he resumed his outing, strongly resolved to reach his target. He tiptoed past the palisade fence that gave the Land Rover house a view of the stream and went to the servitude.

Suddenly, he saw a spotlight in the distance and dashed into the middle of the servitude. The municipality had not cut the grass for a few months and he crawled in for cover and lay on his belly, his head throbbing with tension. He heard the security car slowly making its way on its patrol, searchlight sweeping this way, then the next. Thaba lay flat on the cold, wet grass and kept his head down, shit scared. He dared not run for it, in case the guards shot at him.

The security van drove down to the stream, its tyres making a squishing, crumbling sound on the gravel as it rolled a mere metre away from him and past him, before turning towards the other end of the servitude and heading back up to Umhlanga Road. The spotlight kept sweeping to and fro and, as the van reached one of the houses with its back to the servitude, a powerful motion sensing light came on, projecting its bright light across the servitude.

A giant owl swooped out of nowhere and, just as quickly, rose out the tall grass near him, a rat between its claws. Thaba nearly shat himself but could not run. He banished all superstition of owls to the back of his mind. His son was hungry!

The security van paused for a moment and then slowly carried on towards the tarred road, its light fading as it went. Darkness returned and, after the engine of the security van had revved up in acceleration on the main road, silence returned to the servitude. Thaba cautiously got up and stared at the electric fence and then the back wall.

He searched around for a sizeable rock, took off his wet t-shirt and wrapped it around the rock before smashing it into one of the wall panels, which immediately cracked. Next door to the Land Rover house, a dog barked a few times. Thaba took cover again, until the dog stopped barking. He approached the wall to examine his handiwork, his ears peeled for any unusual sound. There was a huge crack in the wall panel. Painfully, he squeezed three fingers in to the gap and pulled back. He nearly yelped as he pinched his fingers when the two slabs came together, but he persevered after chipping away a small piece.

The hole allowed him greater purchase and he slowly pulled away part of the slab, before pulling the other away. Then, very gingerly, he stepped into the back yard and for a moment marvelled at the size of the garden. In one corner was a vegetable garden, then all manner of flowers and palm trees, before it gave way to a lawn and large swimming pool facing a gazebo. The pool's blue lights shone softly, giving the garden a fantasy look. The security lights did not cover the entire garden and he crept along the wall towards the house. His aim was to reach the kitchen, where from a distance he'd often seen the lady of the house moving around.

He crept closer and closer until he was suddenly jolted out of his mission impossible by the startling sound of the alarm going off into the night sky as the beams picked up his movements. Dogs started barking everywhere instantly and Thaba, stunned by how loudly the alarm pierced the night sky, turned and ran blindly across the garden, almost falling into the pool and smashing his knee on a stone sculpture. He screamed out loud, tears coursing down his face, stumbled into a thorny aloe and clambered through the hole in the wall, landing in a heap on the other side before gathering himself and part running, part limping back to the river. He splashed his way across as the security van's spotlights appeared at the top of the servitude. He fell in a heap on the other side of the stream, lying in the wet mud, too scared to move. As the security van drew closer, its search light sweeping the bank, he crawled in the mud towards the camp. He decided to run for it as the security van's light began to sweep towards his position and he burst back in to his shack dripping wet and wild eyed, only to find his wife sitting up anxiously. He had never felt more ashamed in his entire life.

"Where are you coming from," she asked angrily, needlessly, more out of fear for his safety than any other concern.

"Nowhere," he replied harshly as he flopped beside her, wincing in pain. He pulled off his mud-splattered clothes and put on some damp ones. He pulled the thin blanket they shared over him, turned his back and slept away his shame. Across the stream, the alarm was switched off and an uncomfortable silence descended on the shack.

Two hours later, Marcus got up, brushed his teeth and popped an Ethiopian coffee capsule into the machine. He had been unable to sleep straight after the alarm had gone off, waiting for armed response to call him. He had peeked through the window, not seen anything and decided he was not going to go outside to let them in.

So he told them on the phone that everything looked okay, gave the password upon request and went back to sleep.

He saw the hole in the back wall as he stepped out to the patio, coffee in hand.

"What the fuck... Thandi!"

His wife came running out at the tone of his voice. He was striding towards the wall and he turned dramatically and swept his hand out like a ringmaster after a particularly impressive trick by a lion. She opened the WhatsApp group for the boom area and typed in: "Attempted break-in last night. The fuckers broke one of the wall panels."

All decorum on the group went away each time the issue was crime. A chorus of oh nos, shoot them all, wtfs and are you okays flooded the chat group.

After all the emotion had died down, Marcus turned to the question of the gaping hole in the wall.

"Does anyone know whether builders are considered essential services? I need to fix the wall."

Someone suggested that there was private supplier based in Linden and that, if he were willing to pay the electrician whom they all used on the street, he could use his essential service letter to get there and bring back the panel. Marcus thanked the neighbour for the suggestion, took a photo of the gap and another of a panel before calling the electrician. The neighbourhood tended to use the same service providers to minimise security risks and also secure better pricing.

"Hello…"

"Hello, Givemore, how are you?" The electrician was a Zimbabwean

"All good thanks, sir. How are you?"

"We are fine, thanks, but I have a minor problem and I believe you can help me. I believe you have an essential services letter?"

"Yes, I do. How can I assist?"

"It is a bit awkward, really, but I can't think of any other solution. We almost got broken into yesterday but thankfully they did not get in. However, they broke the wall and I have to get it replaced. There's a guy in Linden who supplies the wall and I sent him a picture and he says he has some panels in stock. Do you mind if I pay you a call out fee plus the cost of the panel into your account and you collect and deliver for me?"

Givemore agreed readily. The people in the boom area in Twinstreams were good customers and always paid promptly. Besides, business was down because people were putting off repairs out of fears of Covid-19. They finalised the arrangement and a couple of hours later he was calling at the boom to be let in. Marcus had already mixed some sand and cement, while his sons watched in fascination. They had never seen him lift a shovel before and now he was gardening and fixing walls. The lockdown was having a strange effect on people. Givemore offered to assist and Marcus gladly accepted.

The wall panel inserted, they poured some cement into the groove and looked anxiously at the sky, hoping the rains would not resume and the cement would set. Thandi emerged from the house, tray with omelette, pot of tea and orange juice in hand, and invited Givemore to have a bite to eat before he went on his way. They ate while Marcus made small talk, asking how business was since the lockdown and at the same time lamenting the crime in the country.

After Givemore had left, he decided to do some gardening since the rain had stopped and the ground was good and soft. They had bought seeds and seedlings as soon as Marcus had announced a previously unknown affinity for gardening as a lockdown project. He summoned his sons from their headphones and laptops and brandished a hoe while his wife watched, trying not to laugh.

"Do you know what this is?" he asked them, like a father introducing his sons to golf irons.

"It is a gardening tool," they ventured.

Marcus made as if to roll his eyes. "Of course! But what is it called?"

The boys shrugged.

"It is called a hoe."

The boys burst out laughing, "Like in hip hop?"

Marcus sighed as his wife joined in the laughter before sternly telling the boys that was not a good word to use after Marcus glared at her.

"Come with me. I want to show you something that I used to do when I was young."

The boys looked at their mother in alarm, but she shrugged. She was enjoying this. They spent too much time in front of their computers and hardly left their rooms except to come and feed themselves or ask what was for supper.

Marcus walked to a corner of the garden the boys had never really set foot in and pointed to a patch in the ground, where his wife ran her vegetable and herb garden. He raised the hoe over his head and the blade flew down the handle towards his wrist. He put it down quickly, before it hurt him.

"Lesson one," he turned to the boys sheepishly. "Make sure you fix the end properly otherwise that will happen and the skin between your thumb and fingers will be pinched really hard. It is a pain you will never forget."

He found a small piece of splinter, thrust it between blade and wood and gently tapped it in. He began to dig while the boys watched, exchanging amused looks. He asked one of them to go and fetch the garden fork and spade from the shed and, after they'd returned, he put them to work on the compost heap. One thrust the fork in the ground and turned up the soil, while the other brought the rich black soil to the patch where he was digging a large, square area. He could see they were struggling. He was too, but he did not show it. He waited to catch his breath, while he pretended to wait for the next shove full of soil. This was harder than he remembered! After getting three more shovels of black soil, he mixed it up with the soil he had dug up and then deftly made some rows.

"Read the back of these," he instructed, handing them the seedlings packets. The instructions told them how many seeds to plant, how far apart and how deep to plant them. They planted carrots, onions, Swiss Chard and Kale, and transplanted some tomato seedlings that his wife had already planted before. His wife, who had been watching, went away and came back with her pail. She proudly and skilfully poured water gently over the areas they had planted and promised to make them a nice lunch.

"It is okay," Marcus interrupted. "The boys and I will braai." He was clearly in the mood. The boys groaned and she laughed. The attempted break-in was forgotten.

Across the stream, Thaba refused to leave the shack, despite the sun having come out. He was stewing in his anger. How did they know he was in the garden? What triggered the alarm? How did that thing work? He cursed the unfairness of life and cursed the rich. Boitumelo quietly took their things out of the shack and laid them out to dry as the other families were doing. The small group of people worked silently, shaking the raindrops off the branches of small shrubs so that they could place their wet clothes on them. The ground was still soggy and muddy and there were worms wriggling about, so they had to watch their children carefully as they liked to pick them up. Thankfully, it was warming up and they could regain a smattering of dignity.

VI

Lusikisiki

Why can't we roam (oh-oh-oh-oh) this
open country? (Open country)
Oh, why can't we be what we wanna be? (Oh-oh-oh-oh-oh)
We want to be free (wanna be free)
Three o'clock roadblock curfew
And I've got to throw away
Yes, I've got to throw away
A yes-a, but I've got to throw away
My little herb stalk!

BOB MARLEY – 3 O'CLOCK ROAD BLOCK

Babalwa eased back in to the settee and said, almost defensively, "I am very proud of where I come from".

"Of course, we all should be…" encouraged Mlibo, taking a sip of his beer.

"Well, I was born in Lusiksiki."

"Best weed in the world!" Mlibo raised a high five.

"Don't interrupt – born into a family of five, well, two and three actually. My little sister and I are from my father but the other three are from another man after my father left and never came back without any warning."

"What? Just like that?"

"Yep, got up one morning and told my mother he was tired of her and he was leaving."

"Goodness!"

"It happens a lot…"

"Yes, but what did he say to you, the children?"

"Our opinion does not really count. I was in Grade 8 then."

"And the other two kids?"

"We had a kind neighbour who helped us with food after my father left and my mother was struggling to make ends meet…." Her voice trailed off. She gave a short laugh and continued. "So, this guy had lost his wife when she committed suicide after being raped and he had never remarried and did not have children."

"What, raped?"

"You know we have a lot of crime in South Africa and Lusiksiki is pretty bad. There are these nyaope boys who seem not to have been raised by human beings. They prey on women collecting firewood, even grannies. It is not safe for any women to fetch firewood alone. They have to go in groups and even that does not guarantee safety. But it is not just poor people involved in crime. There are also wars for business. There's an owner of a service station who was shot when I was growing up. Some people claim it was by a rival in the industry, but there was no proof. Anyway, we live with crime every day from rape to armed robberies and some women don't survive the memory of being raped and sometimes end up killing themselves."

"Fuck…" Mlibo quickly corrected himself at the inappropriate use of the word to express his shock. He took her hand. "Sorry, I mean this is terrible. You know, I know a lot about rape in the townships here in Johannesburg, especially in places where a community shares a few toilets. We get patients at the hospital all the time and it is part of my training to talk about how we would handle such cases from a medical point of view… but raping grannies!"

She glanced at him as if to ask in which country he had been living since childhood but did not say anything. Mlibo tried to change the topic. "You said you were in Grade 8 when your dad left. Where did you go to school?"

"It is called Zamekile Secondary School. It used to be a mud school."

"What is that?"

She gave him the quizzical look again. "It is a school built from mud, you know… sticks and mud, like the old rondavels? Don't you have a village?"

"Sorry, carry on."

"Anyway, one day, some big trucks arrived and we were all moved into these temporary structures – I think they called them mobile classrooms or something like that – and we were told the government was going to build us a new school. We had heard rumours of government building lots of schools but we didn't know whether it was true until they came to our village and moved us in to these prefabricated buildings that were assembled in a matter of days.

"Then the big trucks started arriving with lots and lots of bricks, but when it rained it was tough for them because our roads were terrible. One time, a truck driver just offloaded a whole load of material on top of the mountain, saying his truck was going to be damaged. The guy building the school had to go to and fro several days with his little bakkie to bring them all down to the site. My mother got a job there for twelve months, while most of the building took place. Someone taught them how to lay bricks…" she smiled, "and now my mother can build anything if you just give her directions!"

"Do you want another drink?" She had downed that cider pretty quickly.

"Yes, please."

Mlibo went to the kitchen and came back with another cider. She smiled and said thank you. Normally it was, "Bring me another beer," from her boyfriend. Mlibo sat down.

"Anyway, long story short. One day we were given the date of the official opening. I was a drum majorette, so we rehearsed marching and singing the national anthem. It was funny because everyone struggled with the Afrikaans words and we didn't even think the teacher knew what they meant, but we sang the sounds anyway."

They both laughed.

"On the day of the opening, everyone was dressed up. The old men in their hats, jackets and ties and the women in Amapondo dress."

"Amapondo… Is it true that…"

"Don't interrupt. The women decorated their faces and wore our traditional dresses. My mother looked so, so beautiful and happy! The government paid for everything and there was this tall, dark government guy from Limpopo speaking broken Xhosa who was running everything a day before the opening. I think his name was Thabang or something and he was giving orders left, right and centre, but in a nice, funny way…"

She imitated him. "Principal! Hey Principal! Hey *bantwana, izani lapa*! *Hey wena*, I will fire you, what are you doing?

"Service providers came with a big tent and large music speakers, and they even brought in a team of people to cook for everyone, and they bought all the food from the village, except the vegetables. I think they slaughtered two beasts and the community donated some of their sheep because they knew other villages would come to join in the celebrations. Then, when the minister came, oh my God!"

Mlibo laughed aloud at her enthusiasm. He was glad she was talking about a happier topic.

"I had never met a minister before and I was the lead majorette. Someone saw her big silver car coming in a cloud of dust and shouted '*Nangu uMinister*!' Thabang said he was talking to her on his mobile phone and everyone marvelled at his power. 'Principal, SGB, *izani, izaaaani*!'

"I was so proud. We did our march and salute as the car drove in, followed by two police cars. A policeman opened her door and the Minister came out of the car. He saluted and I saluted too. She smiled, came straight to me and gave me a hug. My mother and the other ladies went crazy shouting, '*Halala! Haaaalaaaala!*' Then they all went into the staff room to talk with the Chief, SGB and some teachers, while Thabang told us to go the tent shouting, '*eTentini!*'

"Afterwards, the minister made a speech, my friend read out a poem and our dancers performed our local dances. Then we all ate like we had never eaten before in a single meal. At the end, when the minister was leaving, the people were singing, 'Oh Zuma yeah, my president!'."

Mlibo smiled broadly. "My home boy! Now I remember. It is true that he started that whole programme of building new schools. You guys in the Eastern Cape got most of the schools."

"Yes, but later I found out they built these schools everywhere in the country. You know, I come from a poor village, but our school had science labs, computer labs, dining hall, a library. It was a proper, proper school with a fence, large clean classrooms… For once we very proud to go to school."

"What is Lusikisiki like?"

"Oh, it is so, so beautiful! It has to be the most beautiful place in the country. We have the sea, these mountains with waterfalls, deep green valleys and very fertile soils. But our people don't farm like those Zimbabweans. Our plots are small and usually for the family. We had Zimbabwean teachers for Maths and Science at our school and in other schools. At the weekend, they showed us films of their long fields. Our teacher even taught us the name of their fields, '*Minda Mirefu*', a name I will never forget. They always used to say, 'We are sons of the soil'. It made some of the other villagers jealous but the Chief protected them. I asked my teacher to teach me how to say my field and he said, '*Munda Wangu*'. That is what I am going to call my daughter one day! My mother said I should marry a Zimbabwean man but you never know!" She locked eyes with him and broke out in to peals of laughter.

He leaned forward and kissed her softly. Her head swam a bit and she couldn't tell whether it was the drink, the kiss or a combination of both. He sat back and asked how she'd ended up in Johannesburg.

"Well, after secondary school, I went off to University in Mthata. It was the first time I was leaving Lusiksiki since that childhood trip to Johannesburg. I had forgotten about the bends…"

"Sorry, the what?"

"Road bends. Lusiksiki is high in the mountains and you drive down the coast to Port St Johns before turning to Mthata and the road is a winding one. It has one hundred and thirty-three downhill bends!"

"One hundred and thirty-three! Are you sure?!"

"Yep! You can see for yourself if you want to visit."

"What, when my people come to see your people," he teased.

"Don't tease me," she replied, pouting. They both laughed again.

"Anyway, after the bends, you come across the massive Umsombovu River. It is like a huge brown snake moving down from the mountains and at some point, just before the turn off and the bridge, you see it pushing itself into the ocean. It turns the ocean brown for quite a distance, it is that powerful." She sounded quite proud of it.

"By the way," she added, as if in an afterthought, "Port St Johns is where I lost my virginity".

"Do tell…"

"There was a music festival called River Fever which brought together a lot of Eastern Cape musicians at Second Beach every year. We travelled as students down from Mthata and spent the weekend there. One thing led to another and so..." She held her palms upwards and outwards and shrugged.

He seized the opening to ask a potentially awkward question. "Incidentally, I heard that in your culture visitors are given a friend, for the night...?"

It was her turn to tease him. "What do you mean?"

"You know, a woman to keep him company... I hear it is an Amapondo thing..." His voice trailed off

She laughed and said she had heard about it and that it used to happen long ago. It was no longer a practice, she confirmed.

"Why, you need looking after?"

He smiled and reached out for her.

In the morning, Mlibo stretched and smiled lazily. What a romp the night before! He was tempted to wake her up and ask for more but he had twenty-one days ahead of him, assuming no natural biological interruptions. No rush! He got out of bed quietly. She stirred but did not wake up. He checked his phone. There was a message from his girlfriend saying she had arrived safely but was immediately going with her family to their cottage in the mountains near Ceres. The cell phone reception was not great there, but she would be thinking about him all the time.

There was a message on the other phone with the new number from the unregistered sim card he had bought. Someone wanted three six packs of beers and another wanted a bottle of whisky. He grinned to himself and said, "Genius!" as he turned the shower taps on with his free hand. He replied to the messages quickly, while he waited for the water to get warm, placed the phone on the bathroom counter and stepped into the shower and turned the water up.

Babalwa woke up when she heard the shower in the bathroom. She sat up a little guiltily. Was she expected to make breakfast? Her mother and aunts had always told her that a woman must always wake up before a man and prepare his food. She decided to wait in bed. She stretched luxuriously and reached for her phone and sent exclamation marks to her friend and promised to get in touch later in the day.

Mlibo walked back in to the bedroom and said, "Morning, Ma Mpondo," and kissed her on the lips. "Did you sleep well?

"Yes, thanks." She kept her lips firmly pressed together because she was afraid of morning breath. She was feeling happy inside. Her boyfriend hardly said good morning, merely grunting some unintelligible sound.

"I have to go the hospital for a couple of hours. There's leftover pizza from yesterday but, if you prefer, there are eggs in the kitchen cupboard. Let me dress and show you. I think I forgot to buy bread. The shops are not closed, so I can pass through later."

She got out of bed, dressed only in her g-string and topless. He felt a stirring within him as she skipped past him, planting her eyes on his, heading into the shower. She left the door open as she brushed her teeth and he watched her ample derrière as she leaned forward to spit into the basin. She caught him looking when she straightened up to the mirror and winked at him. He laughed, put on his t-shirt and asked her to come to the kitchen. A few seconds later, she walked in, still in her g-string but wearing one of his t-shirts. She walked up to him and kissed him properly and then entwined her arm through his as he pointed out the different cupboards and showed her how the gas stove worked.

He went into the garage and, seeing him pack some alcohol into the Jeep, said, "*Hau, kanti*, you take booze to work?"

"No," he replied smoothly. "Remember, I said that not everyone had the chance to buy drinks. I am taking some for the doctors on shift. They will take it home when their shift is done."

"So thoughtful," she said.

"Yeah, well, we have to look after each other. We have heard that doctors in Europe are going through major stress and it will hit us soon. Everyone must come to the party."

Suddenly she got worried for a moment. "You are not going to be treating coronavirus patients, are you?"

"No, Ma Mpondo. For starters, I am not yet fully qualified. We are needed to take up the slack when the doctors are busy. There are still people who will be coming in for other ailments, plus we anticipate GBV cases will go up…"

"GBV?"

"You know… domestic violence. A lot of people," he paused for effect, "men and women, will be trapped with their abusers for twenty-one days."

He got into the car and started the engine, before opening the garage door. "See you in a bit!"

Mlibo drove out onto the road heading to William Nicol and decided against going on to Witkoppen because the Douglasdale police station was right next to it. He drove past Design Quarter and turned right into Leslie. His first customer had given a Juksei Park address. There was no traffic on the road, except the occasional car. He had covered the beers well in the boot in the compartment where the jack and wheel spanner would normally be stowed and had thrown in his medical coat and first aid box casually, just in case! He drove up to a house and rang the bell twice. The gates swung open and he drove in.

A guy came out smiling, greeted him with an elbow bump and said, "You just saved my life, man, but you are not playing with these prices!" They both laughed. He collected the cash, quickly reversed and headed to his next destination. He was going to make a 300% profit by the time he was done. He knew people would be more desperate a few more days into the lockdown. He used the back roads to carry on to Northgate, where he delivered the whisky bottle. The guy there asked whether he didn't mind if he shared his number with his friend. Mlibo told him to go ahead.

He drove to the hospital to show face and ask whether his help was required. He was shocked by what he saw on the way there. The streets in the township were full of people mingling around, not really going anywhere. Neighbours were talking to each other over fences or in the street, while children played with gay abandon. He saw a television crew and recognised a female reporter as she thrust a mic into a group of people, all wanting to share their feelings, presumably on the lockdown. Taxis were driving up and down, ferrying people to heaven knew where. It looked as if the memo had not reached the masses.

The hospital was a massive edifice built during the apartheid years to cater for the black workers who toiled in the mines and kept the apartheid machinery going. He pulled his mask from the glove compartment, carefully put it on and walked in through the entrance, flirted with the nurse at reception and walked to surgery, where his favourite supervisor, a big, gregarious Ugandan man, operated from.

"Is Doctor Okello in?" he asked.

"No, not yet, Mlibo," replied the surgeon's PA. "He is coming in for the afternoon shift."

He flirted with her too, but only when Dr Okello was not around. Dr Okello was this giant Ugandan surgeon who came from a very academic family. He was a huge fan of Lionel Messi but supported Arsenal. The other thing he was crazy about was African food and human beings. His bedside manner was second to none. Despite being a very friendly man who loved his students to bits, he was very serious when it came to professional behaviour. Mlibo could not afford to offend him as his recommendation when he finished medical school would be critical in deciding whether he ended up in a little provincial hospital in the middle of nowhere or not.

He went round the wards and then got back into his Jeep and headed back to the north, taking the highway. Just before he on ramped, he saw two trucks of soldiers off ramping on the other side of the N1, heading towards the township. He cruised down the highway and off ramped again at William Nicol and drove towards the shopping centre opposite Montecasino. Before he walked into the shop, his hands and trolley handle bar were sanitised by a smartly dressed young lady in the supermarket's uniform. His mind went back to the scenes he had just witnessed in the township. He headed for the Deli to pick up some ready-made meals and cold meats. After that, he stopped at the baker for some heat and eat ciabatta and a loaf of sliced bread, before making his way to the butchery, where he picked up some lamb and boerewors for a barbecue as well as a large quantity of biltong. He decided against flowers near the fruit and vegetables sections but picked up a pocket of lemons because he liked lemon with his rooibos tea. In the aisles, he stopped to text Babalwa.

"Tea or coffee?"

"Tea," came the reply.

"What type?"

"Doesn't matter."

He picked up a bigger box of Rooibos. His phone buzzed again.

"And ice cream!" he laughed to himself, picked up a few other items, like yoghurt, paid and put the groceries in the car. He then walked to a small shop that sold purified water and he bought one large container.

Babalwa was on the phone, still relating the previous night's adventures, when she heard the garage door open. She promised her friend she would call again soon and hung up. She had made the bed, cleaned the kitchen and then showered after he had left. Wearing jogging shorts, his t-shirt and his slippers, she had watched two episodes of one of her favourite soaps before calling her friend to share.

She ran to the door leading to the garage as it opened. Mlibo beamed and kissed her. "You are back already," she gushed.

"Oh, so you didn't miss me then?"

"No, silly. I am happy that you are back so soon."

He noticed the television channel was showing a soapie and he frowned slightly. He never, ever watched soapies after watching one many years ago with his grandmother. He found them completely pointless.

"You like soaps?" he asked casually.

"Oh I love them!" she said breathlessly and went on a two minute run-down on the different characters. She spoke of the cruelty, love, weaknesses and greed as if they were real people.

"You know they are just acting, right?"

"Yes, but he is cruel to Nandi," she said of one character. "He must chill!"

"Okay, let me check the news. There's going to be a Covid-19 update at two."

She took the grocery bags from him to go to the kitchen. "Okay, let me make you something to eat."

"No, come and sit with me. This is important. We must all be informed."

She reluctantly joined him. She wondered what the fuss was about. This was just another version of flu, her manager at the bank had said. "We will all be back at work in no time." The bank tellers were worried because, even if they were front-line staff, they had been told to stay at home. Only the senior teller, branch manager and the guy who loaded cash into the ATM were going to the branch, and only for a few hours a day. She dutifully sat next to Mlibo as he changed channels.

The president was not on his own this time. He sat at a large and long desk, a metre apart from the minister of health. The president spoke in general terms before the health minister spoke in specifics. The government was getting it right. Many years ago, during the HIV and AIDS pandemic, the country's most intellectual president to date had spectacularly fucked up because he had been too intellectual for his own good. Such was his political capital that he was still popular to this day. In Europe, he would have probably been forced to resign in disgrace. America was another story. There, bi-partisan politics, not common sense, was the order of the day, even to the detriment of their own country.

The president finished speaking and handed over to the minister of health. This pandemic had helped him banish his growing reputation as an indecisive president. He called it consensus building, but his detractors saw it as dithering. They wanted a strong man after the disastrous, corruption-ridden governance of the previous president. And yet, it was the president's consensus-building and listening skills that had unwittingly helped his reputation. He had listened to the experts from different parts and sectors of the country and had quickly set up a modelling hub. When all the numbers people, the epidemiologists, had given their input and painted a horrific picture, he moved rapidly, addressed the nation and then scored a PR coup by appearing in army uniform to give the army their deployment orders to ensure law and order during the lockdown.

Suddenly the news bulletins and media releases were referring to him as President and Commander in Chief. In Africa, this normally signalled trouble, but this was precisely the time when titles needed reinforcing rather than the other way round. It worked like a charm as all opposition parties fell into line and the middle class applauded his actions. Nevertheless, the NGOs raised questions about how this lockdown was going to be implemented in informal settlements. South Africa vied with Brazil for "most unequal nation in the world" status, but in one country there was a president listening to science and looking for solutions while, in the latter, the nutcase of a president was encouraging social interaction, shaking hands with crowds and encouraging people to go to the beach.

The minister of health presented some numbers. His grave and knowledgeable presentation had the Twitterati pouring out their love for him and declaring how proud they were to be South African. Mlibo wondered what the same people would be saying once the numbers started rising. This whole thing was a game of numbers and, as Indian mathematics professor Vinod K Bhardwaj had pointed out, the real danger in the pandemic would come after the lockdown if it was not done in unison around the world.

Babalwa went to make some lunch while the minister went through the numbers. She had got up as soon as the president had finished speaking. She emerged as the journalists finished asking questions and gave Mlibo his food on a tray. She performed a quick curtsy as he she handed him the tray and Mlibo was pleasantly surprised by this. There were still women who did this! The last time he had seen it was when his father had taken him to visit their village in KwaZulu-Natal!

"So, what's happening," she asked. "Are we all going to die?"

Mlibo laughed. "But I asked you to watch the press conference!"

"I prefer to hear the details from you, honey..." There was no comeback to that.

They ate quietly while he watched the rest of the news. When he had finished eating, she took the tray from him and came back with a bowl of warm, soapy water and again he was surprised. Occasionally, his girlfriend slept over and, when he came back late after a stint at the hospital, she would call out, "Your food is in the microwave!" as he stepped into the house from the garage and then he would have to take his empty plate back to the kitchen and load it into the dishwasher.

He walked into the bedroom and emerged with a little transparent plastic container.

"You smoke weed!"

"Yes, it is not illegal!"

"But you're a doctor!"

"Babe," he surprised himself when he called her that without thinking. "Medical students and doctors will eat, drink and smoke it as long as it is legal. We drink the most beers on campus, smoke the most weed and we also have a healthy appetite in the canteen."

"Wow, why is that do you think?

"You should see what we see in hospital, especially on weekends or public holidays. Stab and gunshot wounds, car accident victims, people injured in domestic violence... It is all very traumatic. As students we study long hours for long years..."

She rubbed his arm up and down, genuinely moved. She took the weed from him and said, "Let me do that. You know we have the best weed on the continent in Lusikisiki."

"Yeah, right. We have Zimbabwean and Malawian students on campus who always compare Binga gold and Malawi gold."

He watched her expertly roll a joint and said to himself, apart from the soapies, he may have found a winner here. He doubted it would last, though. Good for a side chick he thought, but not the real deal. He used to sit and discuss virtually any topic with his girlfriend – from the economy when they watched the inimitable Richard Quest, to the feeding habits of deep sea life when they watched

Animal Planet on BBC Earth and history on the Butterfly Effect on Curiosity Stream. Their favourite discussion was global politics. He enjoyed that the most about the time he spent with her; the sex was good and not necessarily routine. With Babalwa, the sex was brilliant but, when he had asked about her soapies, she had added that she liked to watch the real housewives of Atlanta, wedding shows and the house hunting programmes.

They smoked the joint together and, as the weed took effect, he muted the TV and switched on the Bluetooth speaker. Toni Braxton started singing about a Spanish guitar while he pulled all Babalwa's strings on the couch.

VII

Charity

So much trouble in the world
So much trouble in the world
All you've got to do is give a little (give a little)
Give a little (give a little)
Give a little (give a little)
One more time yeah! (give a little)
Yeah! (give a little) yeah! (give a little) yeah!

BOB MARLEY – SO MUCH TROUBLE

Thandi walked in from the herb garden with some rocket in her hand. She had waited for the boys to almost finish braaing the meat before making a salad. She always struggled to make the three men in her life eat greens, but they always grudgingly obeyed in the end. She quickly put together a salad and brought out some rolls while Marcus fetched the wine, a Vilafonte Series M 2016, from the bar. He lowered the volume two notches on the Bluetooth speaker at her request and immediately raised it back up a notch. She gave him a look and he smiled. She always said he played his music a little too loud, especially when he was doing a braai. He would argue that he needed to hear every single instrument when Ali Farka Toure played duet with other musicians.

"I wonder how the people in the squatter camp are coping," she said, as she eased into the movie-director-style chairs at the patio lunch table.

Marcus paused mid-pour and looked at her. "Are you serious," he retorted. "They could be the ones who tried to break in last night!"

"Yes, you are right," she replied gently.

"So, what do you mean…?"

"Think about it, Marcus. Is it possible they are trying to break in because they are hungry?"

"So we must reward them with food?"

"That's not what I am saying…"

"What exactly are you trying to say, then?"

"That it could be them or it could be someone else. I think we must think of them on two levels."

"Yes," he interrupted, "but, as I said to Sunita, word could get out and before you know it, that camp will triple in size," he protested. Sunita was one of their neighbours, generous of spirit and always wanting to cook a pot or offer to pick up groceries for someone who was too scared to go to the supermarket. She had proposed that the enclosure families help the squatters with food during the lockdown.

She leaned forward and touched his wrist gently. "Hear me out." She put some lamb on her plate, some potatoes and some salad, then passed on the plates.

"Firstly, those poor people don't have any piece jobs because of the lockdown. They don't have money in the bank like you, mister. Then, yes, you must think of security. Do you prefer them to break in because they are starving and then who knows what happens once they are inside? I think we must take up Sunita's proposal"

He waited thoughtfully as he smelled the wine he had just poured. He picked up the smell of ripe raspberries. On many a late afternoon, he took walks with his wife along the green belt and just outside the little gate in their communal electric fence was a house where the owner had planted raspberries. Some of the fruit grew on the pavement side of his palisade fence and the neighbour took pleasure in letting people who were taking their walks or jogging eat their fill. They would stop there and pick the ripe berries and pop them in their mouths, savouring the beautiful taste and staining their hands red in the process. Sun dried, they tasted much sweeter than the ones at the expensive supermarket at their local shopping centre, in which every housewife seemed to show off about shopping. It always took them back to their respective childhoods, when they'd picked the raspberries that grew everywhere but stained their school uniforms purple, for which they'd got into trouble with their parents once they got home. It was always a moment of value-added pleasure to the sunset walks during the week and morning walks on the weekend.

"Okay," he said. "What do you want to do?"

"Well, I can support the appeal on the street group and see who wants to put together a packet of food and then you guys can walk over there and hand them out. It is only a few families and we will be really helping people in need, won't we?" She paused and added for emphasis, "I know all the ladies on the group will agree"

He deferred to his wife's wisdom. Even though she knew he was a committed social democrat in his approach to life, she sometimes accused him of acting just like the bourgeoisie he often criticised. He, in turn, would retort that she did not take security seriously and was naïve.

The subject changed to the lockdown stats coming out of Europe. They had recently holidayed in Florence and had friends in France, a country they visited regularly. The numbers were scary and the fear was what would happen should there be a coronavirus outbreak in the densely-packed townships. This is the reason they had agreed for Londi to go to the Eastern Cape but now they were hearing that people in the province were continuing to go to funerals and football matches in the villages.

After lunch, Thandi replied to Sunita on the street WhatsApp group and said they were willing to contribute to the food parcels for the squatters. Ten other families had agreed to participate and that was enough to agree to hand the parcels over to the squatters on the following day. Marcus volunteered to drive, since they could not cross the racing stream carrying food parcels.

He reversed the Land Rover out of the garage, opened the boot and they loaded the food parcels that Sunita had carefully packed after the ladies had dropped off their respective contributions. "There's enough here for all seven families in the camp," Sunita said.

Marcus thanked her and, together with another husband, they drove out of the boomed area. They had to drive back to the main road out of Twinstreams Central before turning almost immediately back into Twinstreams East because of the way the suburb was planned. However, as soon as they crossed the bridge over one of the streams, they were stopped by police who were waiting for people getting off the N1.

"Where are you going," asked the policeman. His demeanour suggested he was itching to make an example of people who were breaking the law.

"Morning, officer," answered Marcus. "We live straight across here," he said, pointing down along the stream, "and we are heading to the other side of the stream…"

"Why? Are you going fishing?" There was a mocking tone in the policeman's voice.

"No, officer," Marcus kept calm. "I was just about to explain…"

"What's going on?" A burly policeman walked over to join his colleague.

"These gentlemen are going over to look at the river!" the first policeman said to his colleague, clearly relishing the thought of locking up some rich people.

"Is that true?" the burly policeman stood with hand on hips.

"No, officer. I was just about to explain to the officer here. We have squatters who live across the stream from us."

"So?"

"We are going to give them some food that we bought for them."

The burly cop paused. The thin cop smiled and said in a high voice, "Why didn't you say so, man? You know we are locking up people for defying the presidential directive and you know, once I do the paper work, it is difficult to stop the process."

Marcus counted slowly up to ten.

His neighbour piped in helpfully. "Can we show you the food, officers?"

"Let us see, but put on your masks, don't be getting out the car without them. If you don't have masks, you pay a fine!"

The two put on their masks, stepped out of the car and opened the boot. There were seven neatly packed parcels.

"You are not transporting any alcohol?'

"No, officer, none at all."

The burly cop stepped back. He had always wanted to get in to the new Land Rover Defender. "Alright, I will go with you just for safety. You never know how these squatters are going to react when they see food. Let's go!" With that, he opened the back door, heaved himself in and plumped himself on the back seat. "Your car smells nice!" he declared. Marcus and his neighbour looked at each other with a smile. They closed the boot and got back in to the car as the burly cop said to the thin cop, "I'll be back now now, neh?"

Marcus started the car and turned into Acheter Road, towards the stables. "Such a big car and I can't hear the engine! You people live well, neh!" exclaimed the burly cop, laughing at his own comment.

Marcus kept quiet, drove past the sports club on the right and the stables at the left and slowly eased onto the green belt, driving towards the place where the two streams converged. Across from there was the squatter camp. "Yessus, man! Even on the bumpy grass you don't feel a thing in this Land Rover. And your speakers are powerful. I can hear every instrument. Is this that albino guy, Keita something? How much does a car like this cost anyway?" The cop was enjoying his joy ride. Marcus pointed at two houses on the left of the stream.

"That is my house over there and that is his house."

"Oh, I see why you couldn't cross the stream. You would have been swept away. You should be big like me, you could have floated along nicely!" This time they joined him in laughing out loud.

Boitumelo saw the Land Rover approaching and stopping where the two streams met and her heart skipped a beat. She turned to her shack casually and called to her husband to not come out of the shack. Thaba froze and asked why, in a low voice. "The Land Rover guy is here and he has a policeman with him. Don't come out", she hissed. She feared the worst, as she had guessed what her husband had been up to and how he had hurt his knee. Thaba shrank back in the corner of the shack, held his breath and literally started praying to all his ancestors, calling them by name one by one, in the order that his father had taught him, and promising he would never ever attempt to break into a house if he was not arrested.

Marcus, his neighbour and the burly policeman approached the shack dwellers place. The stream had subsided and was flowing gently like a geisha on her slow Sunday morning walk in her kimono. There was a little child playing near the stream and her mother sharply called him over. He ran to his mother and clung to her shabby skirt that hung loosely from her body. The other families stopped what they were doing and stared at the approaching trio. The Land Rover man, a white man and a police officer could only spell trouble.

"Good afternoon."

"Afternoon," mumbled the squatters, almost in unison.

"Who is in charge here?" Marcus felt foolish as soon as the question left his lips

"Nobody," came back the chorus.

"Okay, I…" he checked himself, "We live across the across the stream and we thought with the lockdown we should come and see how we can be of assistance."

The shack dwellers suspicions turned to curiosity.

"This is Officer… huh…"

"Mabhena!"

"Officer Mabhena. He came with us just to see what we are doing. You know, we are not really allowed to go anywhere."

The shack dwellers stared blankly, wishing he would come to the point. "If we could ask the men to please come to the car, we have something small for you."

Boitumelo recoiled. She knew it! It was a trap. "Is it something for the whole family?" she ventured.

"Yes," replied Marcus, bemused.

"Well, then, it is better to give it to the women. We all know men are not responsible."

The portly cop burst out laughing and turned to the two men as if to say, can you believe the cheek of this woman? Marcus was amused and he smiled. "Of course. This way."

The women followed the trio silently to the car, while the men hung back, watching. The women knew all their men's secrets and there was an unspoken solidarity among them. If ever any of their men went for a break-in, they preferred it to be deep inside Twinstreams rather than just across the stream. That way, it could be anyone, even thieves from Thembisa. And, they generally avoided going in groups of more than two burglars. The less one knew, in case of interrogation, the better. Besides, not everyone was interested in burglary. Some of them had part time jobs and only broke into homes when their bosses made some excuse about not paying them.

Marcus turned without thinking to help the ladies across the place where the stream converged but they avoided his outstretched hand and hopped, skipped and jumped across as if they had placed the naturally protruding boulders there for that purpose. He walked round to the back of the Land Rover and opened the boot.

Boitumelo's frown turned to embarrassment first, then a smile. At the back of the car were seven big, recyclable bags all with groceries in them. She looked up in gratitude, felt faint and swooned. Marcus, reached out and caught her by the waist before easing her to the ground. The other ladies quickly moved forward and back to fan her face with leaves they picked up from the ground. She recovered in a few seconds and smiled apologetically.

"These are for your families," Marcus said, while his neighbour and the cop unpacked the groceries.

Boitumelo was in a daze. She wanted to say something but her mouth was dry. Tears welled up in her eyes as she looked at Marcus and his neighbour. "It's okay," said Marcus gently. "We hope this will help."

A chorus of "Thank yous" in Sesotho rang out, followed by one or two "God bless yous" in English.

The trio watched the ladies walk back across the stream, skilfully balancing the bags on their heads while crossing the stream and they got back into their cars.

"You are good people," said Officer Mabhena. "If these people give you any problems, let me know. I will arrest them all!"

They drove back in silence and, as they dropped the officer off, he repeated his gratitude. "Thank you for what you did for those people. They are foreigners, yes, but we are all Africans. Even you, *Mlungu*," he gestured at the neighbour.

"Sharp, sharp!"

Marcus drove back into Twinstreams Central, past the shopping centre, and could not help glancing up at the windows of the local pub, even though he knew it was closed. How great it would be to simply walk in, as was normal practice, and have a beer before getting home. He stopped at the first boom, waved his hand at the electronic key and the boom lifted. They both waved at the guard at the boom and drove through. The tree-lined streets were empty, but he still checked carefully at the T-junction before driving down to their own boom gate that sealed off the road to the eleven houses. He dropped the neighbour off at his house and drove into his own drive. Before he exited the car, he sent a message to the WhatsApp group.

Groceries delivered. Gratefully received.

Thaba heard cheerful sounds from inside his shack and peered cautiously through a gap in the plastic sheet at the entrance. He saw the women walk back into their area with bags. He emerged slowly, a quizzical look on his face. Boitumelo looked at him, a mixture of guilt and relief in her eyes. "They were coming to give us food," she said, in almost a whisper.

"For everyone?" She nodded. There was almost no need for any further words. He took the bag from her and went inside the shack. "Please cut some strong branches and make a table," she said. "We must protect the food this time. Our ancestors have heard our prayers."

There was a moment of awkward silence before Thaba grabbed the axe and went out of the shack. Moments later, she heard the thwacking sound of an axe hacking a tree. She held her son and gave him two biscuits, one more than she would normally give. There was cause for optimism. This food from the rich people across the stream would last them at least one month. Her mind was tormented as what seemed like thousands of conflicting thoughts rushed in to her head. She sat in silence, watching her son in blissful peace, one biscuit in either hand, taking little bites from each side. In the distance, the sound of the axe continued echoing across the green belt.

Across the stream, Thandi watched across the stream as she waited for Marcus to come back. She saw the women walk in single file from where the stream merged into squatter camp. She saw the men smiling broadly and, curiously, she saw one man emerge from one shack and limp towards his wife. They exchanged a word or two before disappearing into the shack. She had a thoughtful expression when she walked back in to the TV room, cup of tea in hand. Her mind was conflicted as a singular thought floated in to her mind. Should she mention to Marcus the thought that had crossed her mind?

Marcus drove back into the yard and, after parking the car, ran into the house.

"How did it go," asked Thandi, concerned.

"All good…"

"And the rush?'

"I forgot I had a zoom call with the guys, like you ladies did." The lockdown was affecting everyone and they needed social contact beyond their immediate families. He took out the laptop and walked towards the bar.

"Secret boys' talk?" Thandi teased, with a quizzical eyebrow raised.

"No, silly," he replied laughing. "You ladies had a zoom tea party, we are having a drink while we solve the world's problems!"

With that, he hopped, skipped and jumped out of the living room, like a teenager happy at the thought of a group chat on camera, beers, wines or whiskies in hand and to hell with the time of day. They were under siege and needed a laugh and a drink!

Their group was called Fatherhood, created after one of them had his first child, a girl. He had walked into the pub and declared he would not tell any more female jokes from that day on. Almost everyone was ready when the call was set up and, before you knew it, they were extending the time to unlimited on the app. The topic started with politics and praise for the president in being decisive for the first time, it seemed, since he became president. After discussing rumours, uncertainties about the duration of the pandemic, a debate on the likelihood of a vaccine being quickly found, their thoughts turned to lamenting the loss of the English Premier League football season. There was much mirth, teasing and the usual boyish clowning around of grown men with children that made their wives roll their eyes every time they all gathered for Sunday lunch. For a couple of hours, it was great to be back in a pub atmosphere.

VIII

Bisho

It's been a long, long time, yeah! (Stir it, stir it, stir it together)
Since I've got you on my mind (oh-oh-oh-oh) Oh-oh!
Now you are here (stir it, stir it, stir it together), I said
It's so clear
To see what we could do, baby, (oh-oh-oh-oh)
Just me and you
Come on and stir it up, little darlin'!
Stir it up, come on, baby!
Come on and stir it up, yeah!
Little darlin', stir it up! O-oh!
I'll push the wood (stir it, stir it, stir it together)
Then I blaze ya fire
Then I'll satisfy your heart's desire. (Oh-oh-oh-oh

Bob Marley – Stir it up

Londi and her cousins were dancing and gyrating to the latest Amapiano hit when one of the cousins spotted the youth pastor's car arriving outside the gate. "Pastor Luba!" she cried and her sister ran to the CD player, quickly ejected the CD and popped in a gospel one. Behind the curtain, they watched the youth pastor get out of the car and straighten his jacket. They giggled and rushed to the kitchen. He walked up to the door and knocked. He waited and knocked a second time. The door swung open and Londi's older cousin exclaimed, "Oh, Pastor Luba, what a nice surprise! Sorry we didn't hear you. We were in the kitchen making lunch and praising the Lord for a wonderful service!"

The youth pastor flashed his gospel smile. "No problem, no problem," he pronounced. "I am so glad to hear that you praise the good Lord while you are working in the house." The girls giggled their thanks as he sat down uninvited. "Do you want some water, Pastor Luba," they cooed. "Or you can try this orange juice that Londi brought us. It is from Zimbabwe but you can buy it in the supermarket in Johannesburg."

"Let me try, let me try," answered Pastor Luba. He was fond of repeating words for emphasis. "The Lord does not counsel against trying new things! I want to add you to the prison ministry. Lots of young people are getting arrested for stupid things and, when they come out on parole, they go ahead and repeat the same offenses and sometimes worse."

"Yes, I heard that guy who was arrested for raping that grandmother in our village was arrested again after he was released and raped two more women collecting firewood."

Pastor Luba sighed. "Yes, there are many cases like that and we need to help the wardens do their work." He paused. "But first, I need you to accompany me to a funeral in East London. As you know, our dear senior pastor is old and, therefore, wise not to travel during the lockdown. He is sending me instead. The government allows up to fifty people to attend and, because of the small number of people, I will need you three to lead the singing at the funeral. He paused for emphasis. "We can't let the departed go without heavenly blessings and music." Then he threw in the sweetener: "We will spend the night at the Beach Hotel for health reasons and then travel back the next morning."

The girls exchanged quick looks.

"Aren't hotels closed because of lockdown?"

"No, they have kept a few open for government business. We get a special permit for pastors going to funerals."

The girls hesitated.

"It is right at the beach and I hear you can see whales and dolphins in the water from your room on the 8th floor," the young pastor added helpfully.

That was enough to generate excitement. The girls were sold. They had never been to the seaside before and, if the Lord called them to service in East London, who were they to refuse? They agreed to travel for the funeral the next day. The burial was in rural Bisho, an hour away from East London, and so they would have to leave early in the morning to make it in time for the service.

"You know how our things take long. The service will start at 10AM. I will share the word of God there, but I have not seen the programme of speakers yet. Then I will also share the word at the cemetery. After that, we will have a late lunch at the homestead and make our way back to East London. I will pick you at 5AM, okay?"

The girls chorused their agreement and Youth Pastor Luba left. They spent the rest of the afternoon trying out their funeral clothes and were a little sad that there would be no after tears party, but the hotel stay would surely more than make up for that? They packed shorts and tank tops, even though they knew they would not be allowed to go onto the beach

"But, you never know, God works in mysterious ways!" Londi's cousins had finished secondary school, just managing to scrape through matric. They had both secured jobs, one after the other, in a clothing chain store on the main road to East London and, after working a few months, had rented a small two-bedroomed house on one of the side roads near Butterworth central, because transport from the village into town was erratic.

They had never been out of Butterworth and were proud of their long-lost cousin Londi, who had come all the way from Zimbabwe, worked in Johannesburg and rented her own little place in Alex. They hoped to travel there as soon as they found a blesser to help them pay their way. They indulged Youth Pastor Luba because he had a crush on one of them, but they had bigger dreams and their sights were set on the bright lights of Sandton.

"What is a blesser?" they'd asked Londi once.

Londi had told them she could leave her place in the township and in seven minutes be surrounded by buildings with twenty floors and more. She told them about the glittering night life where a guy could spend the equivalent of her month's rent just ordering one round of drinks for her and her friends. "That is a blesser."

Londi had arrived from Zimbabwe as a shy and conservative young maid. She was grateful to Thandi and her husband, who had persuaded her to travel with them after he got the big job in South Africa. They had organised a passport for her and she had driven down with Thandi and the boys after they'd finished school three months later, to go and join Marcus. She could not believe the difference in the roads before and after the border. They had climbed and climbed into the mountains on a beautiful, wide road with "cats eyes" on it for people to see at night if they were driving on the wrong side of the road.

Thandi's old Land Rover TD5, a gift from Marcus for her thirtieth birthday, had glided up the mountains effortlessly, past Musina towards the then Pietersburg and beyond, before sweeping into Johannesburg in the early evening. She had never ever seen so many lights on in so many buildings.

"They are wasting electricity," she had exclaimed involuntarily. Coming from a country where power cuts were the norm, she could not fathom how entire office buildings had lights on when the people had gone home from work. The suburbs were laid out like in Zimbabwe and the sizes of the houses and gardens were just the same, but it was the way the city council collected the bins like clockwork on the same day of the week that amazed her. Then there was this recycling thing. They gave you three different bags: one for foods, a second for plastic bottles and the last one for glass bottles!

After a few months, she had made friends with the other maids and was surprised that almost all of them were Zimbabwean. Some of them were qualified teachers, others had diplomas in marketing and there were even a few nurses, who were struggling to join the South African medical system for some complicated reasons that did not make sense. Some of the maids did not "live in" with their employers and preferred the freedom that living in the township gave them.

One weekend, they invited Londi for a weekend out and she had gone to Alex. On Friday night she had discovered Sandton, when they had taken her to a club, where they sat and sipped one cider until a group of guys came and offered to buy them drinks.

"Don't be daft!" her friends told her. "Take the drink," they whispered as she hesitated. "Relax and have fun!" And so it started.

The next day, they went to watch a soccer match at FNB Stadium with some other guys, but these were township boys and they did not spend as much as the guys at the club the previous night. They smoked weed openly in the stands. Londi tried a couple of puffs, but it made her cough and feel dizzy. On the Sunday, she discovered the *chesa nyama* at a huge barbecue place where the music was loud and where the rich boys from the suburbs came back, in their huge, flashy cars, to claim their *kasi* ghetto credentials. She recognised some of them from Friday night at the club.

"You see, that guy likes you, Londi. You go with him to his place, have a good time and drink Moët and he will give you taxi fare in the morning, plus some money for you to do your hair." Londi went back to work in Twinstreams early Monday morning instead of Sunday afternoon as she had promised. And she never looked back after that. A couple of months later, she shyly asked Thandi whether she could move out and stay on her own, promising never to be late for work.

Her cousins loved her stories. She described one shopping mall she called Sandton City, which was bigger than the whole of Butterworth central. "Of course, if is a city, it will be bigger than Butterworth," her cousins would respond and Londi would painstakingly explain that it was not a city per se, but a huge shopping centre. This was met with incredulous looks but she would press on and tell them about wide avenues, people walking their dogs and paying for horse riding near her employers' house. Her cousins would draw the line at that one. Who in their right mind would pay money to ride horses when every village near Butterworth had some? But above all, they loved the blesser stories.

Youth Pastor Luba arrived at 5AM on the dot. "Let's go, let's go, ladies," he intoned breathlessly as he took Londi's older cousin's bag to the boot. Londi and her younger cousin exchanged conspiratorial looks and smothered a giggle. They checked that all windows and the back door were closed again, got into the car and asked the pastor if he did not mind turning off the aircon. It was too cold in the morning. A few kilometres out of Butterworth, some red writing on a white background loomed out of the morning mist. Someone was trying to send a message to the government about something.

Rhulumente, I am waiting for you! Rhulumente where are you? The people's development cannot wait!

"Who is putting up those signs," Londi's younger cousin asked sleepily.

"It is a local businessman who wants to put up a sports complex and he has offered his land but wants the government to come to the party. His logic is to embarrass the government into action."

Londi piped up. "In my country, he would be arrested for embarrassing the government or, at best, receive a sarcastic visit from the secret service to ask him whether he wants to run for parliament. He would get the message and stop this nonsense."

"It is not nonsense. He is trying to push the government and I know the government will end up listening," Pastor Luba replied softly.

"You know, you South Africans are lucky and spoilt." Londi still considered herself Zimbabwean despite her South African heritage. It was more out of habit and a manner of speaking than a rejection of her new country. "I was shocked when I went to the village and saw there was electricity everywhere. I mean, in Zimbabwe people show off when they install solar power at their parents' homestead in the village and here everyone has power! Then you have a guy complaining about a soccer field?"

"But, Londi, this is what we fought for. The struggle was so that we could all live like your people in Sandton City."

Londi laughed out loud and raised her voice. "*Hey wena*, you all have a long way to go. First you have to take your land back!" They all laughed and the car fell silent as the sun began to rise. First there was a beautiful streak of golden light, almost a single ray that pierced the sky as the road wound its way down to the Kei River. Going in the opposite direction, Audis, BMWs, VW GTis and Jettas were racing up, as if they were in a race to reach the top of the hill.

"Why do VW people drive like that?" she asked no one in particular before answering her own question. "It is like people get possessed when they get into any VW, especially Golf, Polo and GTi. You see them in Joburg from traffic light to traffic light or on the M1."

As they descended further, there were goats climbing up the side of the valley in almost vertical fashion, heading for the sweetest dew-fed blades of grass. They looked like ladies in high heels who were not afraid of heights. Londi marvelled at how nimble they were, especially when she saw houses way below in the valley and wondered how on earth they got there. She was about to ask the question but stopped when her cousins gasped. The Kei River bridge appeared before their eyes in the distance, a rust brown colour as they drove towards a Shell Ultra City garage on the right. Pastor Luba slowed down to allow them to enjoy the view and also to turn in to the service station.

"Coffee time, coffee time, ladies!" he announced gaily. He parked opposite the entrance and the girls stretched languorously out of the car and started posing for photos. "Aaaah, I can't see myself," they complained. "It is because you are backlit," offered Youth Pastor Luba, "but it makes for very nice silhouettes, no?"

They walked into the service station. It was busy at this early hour already and the girls headed to the toilets first. When she emerged out of her cubicle, Londi noticed that the ladies were washing their hands rather too quickly. She squeezed the soap dispenser, turned on the warm water and started singing the happy birthday tune. Her cousins shrank in embarrassment as everyone stopped to look at this young lady. Some older lady cheerily said, "*Hey wena mtwana*, it is your birthday?" The other ladies laughed.

"No, Mama. With this coronavirus, we must take our time and wash our hands properly. The government says we must take the amount of time it takes to sing this song."

The lady frowned, hands on hips. "Even up to how old are you now?"

Londi smiled gently, "No, mama. Just the first stanza."

The older lady smiled broadly in only the way that Eastern Capetonians could, walked back to the tap and started singing. The other ladies laughed, Londi's cousins included, and all walked back to the tap and rendered a harmonious version of the happy birthday song.

"Beautiful," cheered Londi and everyone laughed and trooped out of the toilets.

Youth Pastor Luba looked bemused when they found him waiting for them in the common area between the toilets. "Did I just hear someone singing happy birthday?"

The girls laughed and simply replied, "Let's get coffee". Youth Pastor Luba obediently followed them into the cafeteria. They joined the short queue ordered their coffees and sandwiches, paid and left. Youth Pastor Luba drove out of the service station, waited for a gap and turned on to the N2 again. He slowed at the bridge for the girls to have a good view upstream and downstream, but the policemen manning the roadblock just after the bridge waved him forward. They didn't like people lingering on the bridge. He accelerated up and away from the river.

"We are going back above sea level," he proudly announced, turning to look at Londi's older cousin. She smiled like a young princess in a beauty pageant and the two in the back exchanged a furtive, naughty glance again. As they approached East London, they saw signs to various seaside resorts and they were getting excited. Suddenly, something white seemed to rear up in the middle of the road. Londi's older cousin, sitting in the front, let out a yelp and pointed. "There's something on the road!"

Youth Pastor Luba laughed and reassured her, "It is just a wind turbine."

"What is it for?"

"For electricity generation."

"Really! How?"

"Same principle as in a hydroelectric station. You did that in Geography, right? This time, instead of water, it is the wind that generates the power to turn the turbines."

As they got closer, a whole field of wind turbines, giant blades gleaming white on either side of the highway, appeared. The girls were amazed by their sheer size. "But don't the birds get confused?"

"I don't know!"

"Eish, these white people..." began Londi's older cousin.

"Who says it is white people who invented them?"

She kept quiet. It was something she had never thought of at all. The question niggled at her as they cruised in to East London.

"Wow!" cried the girls as a large squatter camp rose out of the sky above the highway. "Shacks with a view! Can they see the sea from there?"

Before Youth Pastor Luba could answer, the girls were being wowed again, this time by a beautiful blue and yellow building that emerged on the same side of the road but further down. "And what is that?"

"That is Clifftop Casino. It is a den of iniquity and gambling. We are not going there." Youth Pastor Luba's curt tone surprised them. He quietly exhaled in relief. They did not argue and he was grateful. He could not afford that place. The last girl he had taken there had gotten carried away and he had had to dip in to the church offering he had received at yet another funeral to cover himself. He did not wish to make that mistake again.

As they swept past the girls asked, "Aren't we already in East London?"

"We are heading first to King William's Town, then Bisho. We can't afford to be late for the funeral. It is not far from here."

Less than an hour later, they were driving into King William's Town. Londi's older cousin spotted a sign that said Steve Biko Centre. "Wow, I knew he was Xhosa but I didn't know which town he came from!" She turned to Londi to add, "You know, our people gave the world Nelson Mandela, Oliver Tambo, Steve Biko, Thabo Mbeki, Zahara…" the girls in the back burst out laughing. "Why are you laughing? Xhosas are everywhere when it comes to excellence. Look at rugby, Siya Kolisi, and when it comes to music, it is countless stars. Every year we have a new music star from the Eastern Cape!"

Youth Pastor Luba turned right and drove uphill away from King William's Town and in minutes they were entering Bisho. He pointed out the monument to the Bisho massacre and other buildings as they drove on the main road.

"This is a strange place," ventured Londi. "It is like a non-town, like someone just dropped buildings from the sky in different places."

They turned silent as the car turned off onto a gravel road after a sign proclaiming "Frankfort", went down a dip towards a narrow bridge, pausing to let a flock of sheep take their time to move off the road. One of the sheep stubbornly stood there until Youth Pastor Luba nudged it on the nose with his bumper. They came across a sign that said *German Graves* pointing off to the right and, on Londi's enquiry, Youth Pastor Luba explained like a history teacher. "You saw the sign that said Frankfort? Just there, where we turned off? There are places called Stutterheim and Berlin around here. It comes from Germans who settled here during colonialism."

"So they had their own special graves?"

"It looks like it… ah, here we are"

Just ahead of them was a village with a white tent erected near the road. There were people standing by the roadside, watching the house as if waiting for a signal. Youth Pastor Luba parked on the verge, next to a Toyota Land Cruiser V8. He wondered whether the local member of the parliamentary legislature was also there. The girls covered their hair and put on shawls to cover their shoulders, in keeping with the demands of the church and tradition, but cleavage was optional. They retrieved their hats from the back of the car, for what was a woman without her hair covered? They walked into the homestead at an appropriate pace, that showed empathy with the bereaved. They briefly greeted the people in the yard outside, muttering polite sounds of condolence before being ushered into the house. In the corner of the small sitting room was a big white man, clutching a bible in his hand.

"Luba!" The voice boomed out as if at a Hollywood soiree. The big white man rose to his feet and embraced Youth Pastor Luba in a bear hug. "Praise the Lord to see you healthy and well. Praise Guaaard!" Youth Pastor Luba was delighted to fall in to the embrace of the man who had given him a scholarship to the Texas Fellowship of the Enlightened.

The funeral was forgotten momentarily as Senior Pastor and protégé hugged fondly in a warm embrace.

Youth Pastor Luba introduced the girls as the youth anointing for the funeral and the big man from Texas immediately declared they should prepare for the Lord's blessing and anointing upon the trio to lead the bereaved in divine worship. "Let's huddle together in prayer." The Pastor started praying aloud, his voice rising with every "Thank You, Jeeeesus," and, as his voice rose and his prayer quickened, so did the spit flying from his mouth. The girls were too polite to wipe it off their faces, especially as it came after every "Jeeeesus". The huddle ended after the devil was nice and bound in prayer. He would not be winning today.

Youth Pastor Luba looked at his mentor with real concern. "What is the meaning of this Covid-19 pandemic, pastor?"

"These are the last days, son. Jesus is coming to take us home."

Londi suppressed a smile. She only went to church because she was with her cousins in Butterworth. In Johannesburg, Sunday mornings for her were either for nursing a hangover or recovering from a night out with the boys. Her mother was very religious and had been telling her about the last days ever since she was a little girl. Her beautiful singing voice came naturally and she enjoyed singing in church with her cousins, but back home she hummed or sang along to Aaliyah instead of choral music. Besides, if the last days had not come in World War I and II, they were not about to start now.

The service in the house did not take long and the girls led the singing beautifully, their harmonies providing comfort to the bereaved. The Lord was certainly present. The pastor from Texas excused himself after the home service, saying he had been summoned to a local government prayer meeting for the afternoon. There was no body viewing because of Covid-19 and the small group walked behind the horse-drawn cart, which ferried the coffin to the graveyard a few hundred metres away. Youth Pastor Luba gave the sermon and prayed for the soul of the departed and asked the good Lord to comfort those who had stayed behind.

"The Lord works in mysterious ways," he told his audience. "These are the last days and our dear departed is interceding right now for us in heaven so that we can all be received when our time comes. Prepare yourselves. The government says, 'stay safe, stay home'. I say to you, stay holy, stay pure. Keep going to the house of worship and the Lord will protect you. Don't ask too many questions, be still and know that God is God"

A chorus of Amens followed. Youth Pastor Luba ended his sermon and the girls led the singing again as the coffin was lowered into the grave.

Young men from the village came forward and began shovelling earth in to the grave. Londi watched in fascination. They worked swiftly, nostrils flared, eyes squinting in concentration, the sweat glistening on their biceps and their body odour mingling with the group. Their shovels made that soft crunching sound as they came into contact with the soft earth and then a thud as the soil landed on the coffin before becoming a soft pillow sound as earth hit earth with the grave filling up. Dust rose into the air and the small group of mourners briefly stepped back. Soon, there was a mound and the young men ceased their labours. One of the old men reached into his pocket and gave them R20 each. They respectfully murmured their thanks and stepped to the back of the group, their shovels by their sides.

The widow, barely able to walk without support, stepped forward and placed some flowers on the mound, followed by her wailing daughter, who nearly collapsed on top of the grave. The other women helped her to her feet and the group withdrew to walk back to the house. At the gate, the visitors were offered a dish of water to wash their hands and then invited for a meal of lamb, intestines and samp.

Londi was mildly amused that everyone ate with a spoon and she was too embarrassed to ask for a fork and knife. She looked around the little sitting room. It reminded her of her mother's little house back at Heany Junction. There was a worn-out yellow sofa for two and a separate armchair where, presumably, the deceased father used to sit while being served his breakfast in the morning, tea at ten, lunch and tea again at three, always on a tray, and he always dressed in jacket and tie with obligatory walking stick by the side.

In between, squeezed into a tight corner, was a display cabinet bought on the cheap. As the name suggests, it displayed their best china, cups and plates, which were reserved for visitors such as the pastor from Texas Fellowship of the Enlightened, but also porcelain sheep, dogs and cats figurines placed on a doily with small red beads around the edges. She recognised the bulldog and poodle from her childhood, but could not name any of the cats. Besides, she didn't like cats. They were associated with witchcraft back in Heany Junction. Opposite the sofa and armchair was an old Sansui television.

They made small talk while they ate and the mood was lighter as the older men in the room reminisced about the departed and how he would scream at anyone who came near his flock of sheep. They laughed out loud when one narrated how they had become friends after the departed had chased him halfway across a meadow, menacing knobkerrie in hand, because his sheep had dared mix with his.

Soon it was time for a final prayer and hymn, this time for the safe travel of the trio. They were offered a sheep, but Youth Pastor Luba politely declined, saying they were spending the night in East London and he would not want the sheep to suffer in the boot of the car.

They drove back in silence, each one preoccupied with their thoughts on death, the meaning of life and whether they had done enough to meet their Maker with pride should they be called home. Occasionally, one of them would sigh and say something. "It was lovely funeral, nice and small." Before long, Clifftop Casino loomed large on the highway and they off ramped and drove into Vincent suburb, on their way to the central business district of East London. Londi's cousins were watching with interest. Vincent was a mixture of large houses and office premises. They went round a traffic circle and the cousins laughed, saying it was funny and dizzy. As they drove on to Oxford Road, the street became busier.

The street was filthy compared to Vincent. The girls gasped in shock. "Why is there so much litter everywhere? This is East London, for heaven's sake!" All the way, right through Oxford Street, there was paper everywhere and the people walked as if they didn't see it. They drove past a small statue of Steve Biko at the Town Hall, past a few clothing stores and fast food outlets. They came to a four-way crossing with traffic lights and Youth Pastor Luba told them that, if they turned right, they would reach the airport.

"Can we go there tomorrow, just to see," the girls cried out.

"We'll see, we'll see," he replied and carried on down the road and, all of a sudden, as the road began to curve, there it was: the ocean!

"Water!" screamed Londi's older cousin, sitting in front. The two girls at the back moved off the back of the seats and sat on the edge to get a better view.

"A ship!" shouted Londi's younger cousin, pointing in the distance as they reached the bottom of the bend.

"Wow," Londi said. "How does that thing stay afloat?"

Youth Pastor Luba cruised slowly along the boardwalk, past a water world park, a huge hotel and conference centre on the left and then past a restaurant that seemed to loom over the ocean. "There it is," he said. There was a large building bordered by a gym and open ground with a huge sign at the top saying *Beach Hotel*. Youth Pastor Luba drove into the small parking lot and announced with a triumphant smile, "Here we are, ladies! Here we are!"

The girls were beaming as they stepped out of the car and walked up the short steps to the hotel reception. There was a desk at the entrance where they were asked to show their hands. A staff member squirted some sanitiser into their hands, while another took their temperature, names and phone numbers.

"This COVID thing is serious!" Londi's cousins whispered to each other.

"What was your temperature?"

"Mine's 35.8. You?"

"I'm 36, ha ha, I am better than you!"

They giggled and walked up to the reception desk, led by Youth Pastor Luba. The staff, dressed in black and white, smiled and gave a cheery, "Good afternoon, Sir!"

He handed over his ID and said, "I booked for the 8th floor." The booking was confirmed and Youth Pastor Luba paid for the single night immediately, saying he would settle meals on check out. They picked up their bags and trooped across the lounge area, away from the conference rooms, to the lifts. The doors made clanging noise as they closed and, with a sudden jolt, the lift began to climb. The cousins laughed nervously and held onto the metal bar while studying themselves in the mirror. Youth Pastor Luba smiled to himself. He wondered why women always did that; briefly study themselves in the mirror and adjust their hair, even when the adjustment was not really achieving anything different from when they'd stepped into the lift.

The lift shuddered to a halt and the doors opened noisily to reveal a neatly carpeted corridor. They stepped out and turned to the right. Youth Pastor Luba had booked two rooms and when they got to 809 he announced, "This is us, you two are next door," as he handed the card key to Londi and her younger cousin.

The older cousin protested feebly, "What do you mean, us?"

Youth Pastor Luba smiled and said, "Is it not written, 'If anyone is worried that he might not be acting honourably toward the virgin he is engaged to, and if his passions are too strong and he feels he ought to marry, he should do as he wants. He is not sinning'?" deliberately leaving out the last sentence in the verse.

"Is that in the bible?"

"Yes, my sister, Corinthians…"

"But we are not engaged…"

"That is the Greek version. The Hebrew version says something else," Youth Pastor Luba smoothly replied, caressing her upper arm as Londi struggled with the card key next door.

"Here, let me do that for you," offered Youth Pastor Luba. He inserted the card key, pressed down on the lever when a green light popped up and pushed the heavy door open. It opened onto what looked like a small lounge with couch and kitchen before leading past an open bathroom door and into a large, airy room with a double bed.

"Oh, wow!" cried the girls, rushing to the window. "Look at the ocean!"

Youth Pastor Luba smiled and let the door close, calling out, "See you in half an hour. Please change into shorts and slippers."

He turned back to Londi's nervous but smiling older cousin. "Come, it is okay," he said gently, opening the door and holding it open for her. She picked up her small bag and stepped into the room. Youth Pastor Luba grabbed the remote and absent-mindedly switched on the flat screen television mounted against the wall and tuned into a music channel. Londi's older cousin walked to the window and slid it open. A breeze swept into the room and she inhaled deeply.

"I can smell the sea," she half whispered. Youth Pastor Luba came up behind her and put his arms around her, slowly moving them to her breasts. She shivered involuntarily and slowly pulled them down. "So, what is the plan?" she asked

"Change into shorts and go and take a walk on the beach before temperatures start falling," he replied.

She walked to her bag, opened it and pulled out a t-shirt and shorts. "Turn around."

Youth Pastor Luba was about to say, "There's nothing there that I have never seen before," but thought better of it. He mimicked a sigh, turned around and gazed at the ocean. He couldn't believe how easy it had been. He had expected greater resistance to sharing a room from Londi's older cousin and even from the other two. But the way they had giggled suggested his fancying of the older cousin had been noticed and appreciated.

"I'm done."

Youth Pastor Luba turned around and sharply drew in his breath. He had never seen her in shorts before because the church always required their ladies to dress "modestly to shame the devil". He licked his lips in a futile gesture to moisten his dry mouth and she laughed in only the way that a woman who knows can. He felt like he had lost the initiative. She was now in the lead. She closed her bag and he took it from her and put it in the wardrobe.

"Let's get the others…" As she walked past him, he lightly touched her at the waist. She looked at him and he kissed her tenderly. Her heart leapt and her lips quivered ever so slightly as tongue met tongue. Her arms automatically went around his neck and, eyes closed, she returned the kiss passionately. They reluctantly pulled apart after a while and went out the door and knocked on the door of the room next door. It opened almost immediately. The girls had changed into shorts, t-shirt and slippers and were beaming shyly. Youth Pastor Luba turned and led the way back up the corridor to muffled giggling behind him. He was glad, momentarily, that they couldn't see his broad grin.

They rode the lift down to the ground floor and walked out into the mid-afternoon sunshine. They walked across the large piece of open ground, crossed the road and hopped onto the boardwalk. They followed this for a few metres until they found some steps going down to the sand. The girls shrieked, discarded their slippers and ran onto the sand. They were in heaven! The three girls frolicked on the beach, shrieking as the water lapped at their calves and at times saying they were feeling dizzy as they ran.

Youth Pastor Luba watched, amused. He was sitting on the wall between the boardwalk and the sand. He was amused, but not surprised, at the number of selfies they took. He used to do the same when he was on scholarship in Texas at the Fellowship of the Enlightened.

After an hour, it was beginning to get cold and the girls were tired from the early morning rise, the funeral and scampering about the beach. The girls spotted a pub on the other side of the road bordering the beach and asked to go for a drink but Youth Pastor Luba declined saying it was the devil's workshop and besides, they were likely to get their mobile phones stolen there. They walked back to the hotel and Youth Pastor Luba advised Londi and her younger cousin to shower, take a nap or watch some TV before announcing that they would all meet downstairs in the lobby in a couple of hours for dinner. There was no giggling this time, merely an exchange of meaningful looks between the girls.

As they walked back into their room, Londi's older cousin announced she was going to take a bath. Youth Pastor Luba reached in to his backpack and pulled out a small bottle of bubble bath. "I got this for you," he announced almost shyly.

"What is it?"

"It is called bubble bath," he offered. "You pour it into the bath when you run the water. It will make bubbles.

"Oh, like in the movies…"

"Exactly." He stretched the bottle out to her.

She hesitated, smiled and took it from him. In Butterworth, she used a basin to wash in and now she was about to get into a bath tub that was almost the size of their sofa at home. She went into the bathroom, ran the water and did as had instructed. She looked at herself in the mirror, trying to gauge her own confused feelings as the steam rose. She turned back to the tub and smiled when she saw the bubbles rising. She peeled off her t-shirt and dropped her shorts, felt the water temperature and stepped in. As she did that, the door opened and in stepped Youth Pastor Luba, stark naked, his member dangling loose between his legs.

She gasped, took a step back and slipped in the bath, but he reached out a strong arm and grabbed her before she could hit her head. She held onto him for balance and he pulled her towards him. She felt like a leaf, free-floating from a tree in the autumn. He kissed her and she moaned ever so slightly. He eased off and stepped into the bath, his member now as rigid as the rod on the shower curtain. She could not take her eyes off him. He smiled and settled into the water, sitting directly behind her. He cupped her breasts, began lathering her body and she swooned. The heat of the bath, the moment and the fragrance of the lavender bubble bath were all getting to her. She closed her eyes and let herself go.

Two hours later, they stepped out of the lift, hand in hand, and walked towards Londi and her younger cousin sitting in the lobby.

"Let's go and eat," said Youth Pastor Luba keeping a perfectly straight face.

Londi's older cousin's face was glowing as they stepped into the restaurant.

IX

Booming business

It take a joyful sound
To make a world go 'round
Come with your heart and soul
Come 'a come and rock your boat
Cause it's a punky reggae party
And it's tonight
It's a punky reggae party
And it's alright

Bᴏʙ Mᴀʀʟᴇʏ –Pᴜɴᴋʏ Rᴇɢɢᴀᴇ Pᴀʀᴛʏ

Mlibo reached for his second phone as four messages followed each other in succession. He gingerly moved away from Babalwa to avoid waking her up. She was still fast sleep, a picture of beauty, ample chest rising and dropping gently. He opened the messages. All of them were orders for booze. Price did not seem to deter the people making the request and he wondered aloud whether he should raise his prices.

"Mmmmm…?" Babalwa stirred.

"Sorry, I did not mean to wake you. I was talking to myself."

"Who does that?"

He chuckled nervously. "Don't worry about it. Go back to sleep." He got up to go to the bathroom.

"Where are you going?"

"I have to go to the hospital. They need extra hands."

Babalwa sat up. "Let me make you some breakfast then. You need to eat properly and stay healthy."

There was no stopping her. She got out of bed, wearing only her underwear. He loved the way it sat halfway down her buttock cheeks, as if it were a pattern painted onto her body. Nature and fashion design at their best. She put on a long t-shirt that went down to her thighs, walked round the bed and went to brush her teeth.

"Okay, then," he replied and followed her into the bathroom. He showered while she quickly brushed her teeth and went off to the kitchen. He mentally planned his distribution trip while he showered. Fortunately, all the orders were from Bryanston, Lonehill and Sunninghill. Easy to do, he thought to himself. The tricky part would be whether to use Witkoppen, the highway or the back roads.

He decided he would start with the furthest destination and work his way back, like he used to do in the bean bag race at primary school. He dressed quickly in a comfortable track bottom, trainers and cardigan and walked into the kitchen.

"Wow, that looks yummy!" She had made a couple of fried eggs, medium, with a rasher of bacon, and coffee was percolating into a small coffee cup on the coffee maker.

"You look yummy yourself," she replied, smiling. She was delighted that he liked on sight the simple breakfast she had made. Her mother had always told her, the greatest instinct of a woman at the most basic level of humanity is to feed and nurture. She had also warned her that the most instinctive thing a man did, at a most primitive level, was to spread his seed. "*Indoda injalo*," she always used to say. She disagreed often with her mum on many societal issues, especially after she had moved to Johannesburg, and yet always wished she could be even just half the woman her mother was. Her generation seemed to be happier, have less drama and be more caring about family beyond the nuclear family.

"You dress like that to go the hospital." It was more of a comment than a question.

"Remember, babes, all I have to do is put on my white coat and we are good to go. We either wear scrubs or dress like this."

"Okay."

He finished eating, rinsed his plate and cup before placing them in the dishwasher. Again she was pleasantly surprised. Her boyfriend would never, ever wash his plate. Mlibo thanked her, grabbed his key and opened the boot before opening the garage door. He removed the spare tyre cover, stashed some of the high-value day's orders and covered it again. He then got a big case that he had stuck a medical sticker on, put in some drinks in six packs and covered them with a medical coat and surgical masks.

"Are you not putting yourself at risk?"

"No, it is fine. I have a doctor's sticker. They don't stop me."

"But I saw them arresting people on the news…" She had started watching a bit more of the news ever since his jibe at her endless cycle of soap watching.

"I'll be fine. Besides, I always have cash on me."

"Just in case?

"Just in case!"

He gave her a light kiss, got into the car and opened the garage door. As the light streamed in, he glimpsed the gap between her thighs silhouetted in the doorway to the kitchen and smiled to himself. Life was good! He blew a kiss at her, reversed and closed the garage door. He drove slowly out of Tranquil Estate, looking at each house and seeing a couple of curtains part and close just as quickly. His mind went back to the student pub on campus on the night of the lockdown.

"This thing is going to be an interesting study into human behaviour," he had said to the group of students sitting at the bar

"Why do you say that?

"Can you imagine people in complexes and estates cooped up in their homes for twenty-one days, not even allowed to walk within the complex?"

"Either people will kill each other or divorces will go up."

"I hear divorces went up in Italy, a very conservative Catholic country when it comes to this subject," one student chimed in.

"Yep, but how do you divorce and still stay in the same house?"

"Well, it takes a while for the paperwork to be done."

"Yes, but normally one of the parties moves out."

"Then, there's GBV that is going to explode."

"All these guys we treat every morning over the weekend will be frustrated with no booze or cigarettes and they will take it out on their partners."

"I don't get this cigarette ban…"

"What kind of a medical student are you?"

"Yes, but we will just get a flourishing of the underground trade. The same for booze."

"Government cannot make decisions for the good of the public because they are afraid the public will misbehave. If they clearly articulate what the dangers of smoking are in relation to Covid-19, people will just have to be adult and manage. There will be extreme cases, of course, but we are talking pandemic here. Those numbers coming out of Italy and Spain are not just statistics, they are real people with families!"

"You know, you worry about people in your fancy complexes. What about our people in the townships?"

"Again, government must make things as plainly clear as possible for the masses. Funerals and churches are a disaster for them."

"So, articulate for the middle class and plain and simple for the masses?" Everyone had roared with laughter.

As he navigated his way of out of Lonehill, Mlibo smiled at the memory of the conversation. It never mattered what he said, he was always seen as the rich kid in his circles. He decided to avoid William Nicol and drove to Pineslopes Shopping Centre, left into Witkoppen and then short right into Leslie in Magaliessig. He took the narrow street that arrowed down to Main and turned right onto Main, which had almost no traffic. Nevertheless, he sped up to get to Sloane as quickly as possible and darted left when he got there, switched on his GPS and began to look for the first of three addresses in Bryanston. Each time, he drove into the buyer's property, where he offloaded his merchandise, got paid and drove off. Some spouses looked on approvingly, some didn't. He always asked the buyer whether he wanted any ciders or not and that always seemed to win spouses over to his side.

Leaving Bryanston, he cut across Devonshire Park from Bryanston Drive, entering through one boom gate and emerging out of another onto Wilton street. He passed a little traffic circle, got to the traffic lights intersecting Sloane again, peered left and right and drove straight across, past a bigger circle and over the highway into Twinstreams. As he crossed into Twinstreams, he saw the orange and white of a Johannesburg Metropolitan Police Department van at the traffic lights on Witkoppen and Cambridge. His heart skipped a beat but he did not change speed. He avoided looking at them and drove on. He watched his rear view mirror nervously as he slowed at the speed hump on Broadlands Road. The police van had turned left and was heading towards him.

He went over the hump and stopped at the four-way stop, indicated right and turned, heading towards the self-operated boom where you waved your hand at a monitor to get through. The boom rose as the police car also turned in to Lomagundi. Again, he tried not to accelerate. His foot was shaking almost uncontrollably, almost like the day he'd gone for a driving test. He dialled the number of the next buyer and said he was two hundred metres away. The buyer had asked him to ring a number and select option 1. The buyer said he would open right away. In his rear view mirror, the police van came into view again. Mlibo continued at his normal speed while the police van gained on him.

At the bottom of the street, he saw the big gates to a boomed off area begin to open. He headed straight for the gates and drove in as the police van slowed down and turned right into Riverside. He glanced in his mirror and saw the policeman in the passenger seat staring at his car. He could not tell whether he was looking at his car or just looking in his direction. Mlibo drove slowly down the enclosure road, looking at the house numbers until he got the buyer's house.

"I am here," he texted via WhatsApp. The man opened his gate to let Mlibo drive in while he opened his garage for a quick and private offload. As the garage door rose silently, it revealed the new Land Rover Defender and another family SUV parked next to it.

Marcus walked out of the garage as the young man drove into the yard. He regretted not having waited in the queue at the liquor store before the onset of lockdown. He had relied on his stocks but, with nothing to do and no pubs allowed to open, he had surprised himself by drinking more than he normally drank at home. While he still had some wine stocks, he was low on whisky and out of beers.

"Good morning!" He bumped elbows with the young man. "Quite the enterprise you are running there!"

Mlibo grinned widely. "Just trying to help in a difficult situation, Sir!"

Marcus picked up the clipped tones that came from privileged kids. The young man before him was not some pub employee clandestinely selling merchandise on behalf of the owner. He watched as the young man opened a suitcase full of different brands of beer under some white coats and surgical masks.

"Wow, you have all these brands?"

"Yes, Sir. I stocked up as soon as the announcement was made."

Marcus confirmed his thoughts. The young man must have had spare cash to be able to "stock up". He took the three cases of Stella Artois from him and placed them on top of the old dishwasher that he had not gotten around to disposing of and turned back. The young man had just pushed the suitcase deeper in to the boot. He pulled back the spare wheel cover and revealed neatly cushioned bottles of whisky. He pulled out a Laphroaig 10 and handed it over to Marcus.

"Impressive! You don't have a Lagavulin, by any chance?"

"Sorry, Sir, I did not expect anyone to order that." They both laughed. Marcus was genuinely intrigued and the young man seemed to want to linger. "Aren't you scared of the cops?"

"It is a risk worth taking and, if I get caught, I guess we will have talk…"

"You are selling surgical masks as well?"

"No, Sir." The young man hesitated. "The thing is, I am a medical student and I am using my doctor's sticker to get around. So I cover my merchandise with medical apparel to complete the story."

Marcus became concerned. "Thanks for the delivery, young man, but the consequences could be serious for you if you are caught!"

"I know, Sir, but I only go by reference from people I know and so the circle grows. Besides, I am almost out of stock. There has been massive demand almost from day one of lockdown and, fortunately for me, it has been around these areas. The police hardly come to this side of town except to do a slow crawl in the area. They are busy enough trying to keep people off the streets in the townships. Their resources are stretched thin."

"Well, thank you very much. Can I give your number to a couple of friends of mine?"

"Sure! But they must hurry. I am running out and there's a lot of fake alcohol out there. We wouldn't want your friends to get sick ordering from the wrong people." They both laughed as Marcus paid him.

"I will open the big gate for you from here."

"Thank you, Sir, have a good day."

Marcus smiled and walked out to the street as the young man reversed out of his property. The young man smiled, waved and drove off. As he neared the gate, Marcus pressed on his remote to open it. The young man flashed his hazards and accelerated up River View Road towards the boom gate.

Mlibo kept his eyes peeled in case the JMPD patrol van was still in the area. He still had two deliveries to do in Lonehill. When he got to Witkoppen, he made the decision to turn right and dash for it to Main. If he made it to the intersection without incident, he would turn right onto Main and literally be home and dry. The cops were always on Main and Witkoppen after the traffic lights and never down Main road.

There was no traffic on Witkoppen. He sped up the road with its strange middle island that people normally walked on in busy traffic. He slowed down at the traffic lights at St Peter's School but did not stop at the red light, telling himself schools were closed anyway. He drove down towards the Clay Oven squatter camp. It was incorrect to call it that, actually, as the owner of the land had donated it to homeless people. It was prime property, smack in the middle of the northern suburbs, sandwiched between a Porsche dealership and a scattering of restaurants on the one side and upmarket estates on either side. It was fenced off with palisade and Mlibo often saw a church group feeding the residents on Sunday afternoons. He made it to Witkoppen and Main, waited for the green arrow and filtered in to Main. It was all clear down Main and he accelerated again and swung left in to Lonehill Boulevard and right in front of him, at the bus stop, was a JMPD van and two policemen.

"Fuck!" Mlibo swore under his breath as one of the cops motioned him to pull over and stop. Mlibo slowed into the bus stop, his mind racing with questions. Had he replaced the spare wheel cover properly? Did he cover the rest of the beers with the coats and surgical masks after that nice last buyer's house? As he stopped the car, he pulled his stethoscope on the passenger seat more into view as it slid to the back every time he accelerated. The policeman walked directly to his window.

"Morning."

"Good morning, officer."

"Out and about this morning?"

"Yes, sir..."

"I assume you are not going shopping since the shops are behind us and you are coming from Main."

"How do you mean?"

"You would be coming from inside Lonehill, if you were going to the shops."

"Ah, I see. Clever!" laughed Mlibo. "That's how you catch them!" The policeman did not smile.

"No, I am coming from the hospital. I am a doctor."

"You look too young to be a doctor."

Mlibo gestured at his coat and stethoscope.

"Do you have a letter?"

He pointed at his windscreen.

"There's my official doctor's sticker. It has all my details on it."

The policeman asked for his ID.

"I can show it to you through the window, officer. It is safer for you that way. We work with very sick people. We sanitise our hands when we leave the hospital, but..."

The officer quickly stepped back, looked directly into his eyes for a moment and then walked round to the left of the windscreen. He peered intently at the doctor's sticker on the bottom left while Mlibo held up his ID towards the passenger window from inside the car. The policeman dismissed it with a wave of his hand and waved for him to carry on.

"Not good, not good," Mlibo muttered to himself as he drove off. He could still feel the effects of the adrenalin surge in his tummy. "I am not doing this shit again." He quickly made the last two deliveries and headed home. He felt like he needed a second shower or a vigorous round of lovemaking to get rid of the adrenalin in his system. Babalwa would be happy.

X

Johannesburg Dreamin'

Oh why, my head,
In desolate places we'll find our bread,
And everyone see what's taking place, oh
Another page in history
We come from Trench Town,
Come from Trench Town;
We come from Trench Town
Lord, we free the people with music

BOB MARLEY – TRENCHTOWN

Youth Pastor Luba pulled up at Londi's cousins' little house in Butterworth after what had seemed a shorter drive than the one they had taken going down to East London. They had asked for late checkout which had been granted for midday as the hotel, though designated an essential service, was literally empty. They made a quick detour to the small airport, but it was closed. So they looked at the parked aircraft from the main road and Londi's cousins asked how those huge things could possible stay in the air. Youth Pastor Luba had actually driven back to Butterworth slowly, trying to draw out the moment as long as possible.

"Here we are, here we are," he announced unnecessarily. The girls had enjoyed the short excursion but were also happy to be back home. The other two were itching to hear details of the night in the other room at the hotel. They walked into the house with the bags while Londi's older cousin said "goodbye" to Youth Pastor Luba. When she walked into the house the girls shrieked gleefully and led her to the sofa, one on either side.

"Tell us everything!"

While they were unpacking, the radio station announced that the president would address the nation that evening on television. They made supper while they waited and when he came on, about fifteen minutes late as usual, he looked tired, like a man short of sleep and with the world's burdens upon him.

"This man needs our prayers," said Londi's older cousin.

The president spoke for fifteen minutes and then announced that workers who had travelled to the provinces before the lockdown had a window to travel back to their work places as the government would be easing the alert level from 5 to 4. Londi loved her cousins, but Butterworth was too small and she found the constant to and fro between church and home a bit mundane and monotonous. There was Sunday service followed by ladies' meeting, then youth meeting, bible study group, choir practice and, in normal times, evangelical outreach, also known as the great commission. She preferred the work time table and weekend parties in Johannesburg that took her from club to club and braai to braai. She announced to her cousins that she would have to take up the window of opportunity to travel back. She was sure her employer needed her and she didn't want to go back and find they had given the job to someone else.

"But those people love you. They wouldn't do that!" protested her cousins. Her mind was made up, though. As they washed the dishes for the night, she had a short coughing fit.

"Drink some water!"

"Thanks. I think I was talking and trying to swallow at the same time. I think I will go to bed early tonight."

"Yeah, we are all tired. Let's go to bed. We all know some people will have sweet dreams," Londi's younger cousin mocked her older sister laughingly. They all laughed, switched off the lights and went to bed.

The next morning, Londi went on a ticketing app and booked the evening Greyhound from East London to Johannesburg via Aliwal North and Bloemfontein. After breakfast, she helped clean the house and then took the short trip to the village with her cousins to inform her relatives there that she was heading back to Johannesburg. They prayed for her safe return and she returned to Butterworth central to further pass time with her cousins before making her way to the main road to get a taxi to East London.

"It won't be easy to get a lift because many taxis are parked!"

"Yes, people are not travelling."

"Should I ask Luba?"

"Luba!" The two younger girls laughed. "So it is Luba now?"

"Come on, guys…"

"No, I don't think it would be fair to ask him to take me to East London. Only if it looks desperate. There's still time." Londi hesitated. "And please, don't commit to anything with him. You have to see what else life has to offer."

"Yes, I agree," chimed in the younger cousin. "Butterworth is small and there's more to life out there."

"I know, I know…" replied the older cousin. "I want to see if all those stories you have told us about Johannesburg are true."

"Trust me, they are true stories, baby!" Their laughter was interrupted by a car pulling over. They looked at it suspiciously as a young guy rolled down his passenger side window.

"Going somewhere?"

The girls hesitated.

"I am going to East London, if you are waiting for transport," the young man offered.

The girls looked at each other and quickly conversed. Kidnapping, rape and murder of women was common in the country, but time was running out.

"Can we take a picture of your number plate? It is just that only one of us is going."

The guy laughed out loud. "Of course!" He added, "Actually, a very wise thing to do."

Londi's older cousin walked round to the back of the car and snapped a picture of the number plate. The girls hugged and shed tears and the cousins promised to come to Johannesburg after the full lockdown had been lifted, and before Londi's older cousin was permanently snagged by Youth Pastor Luba. Londi placed her bag on the back seat, got into the passenger side at the front and waved goodbye to her cousins.

"My name is Loyiso."

"I am Londi."

"Please put on your seatbelt."

The guy put on his music and drove off. At the end of the street, he stopped next to another person flagging him down, but they were only going five kilometres out of town and he declined to give them a lift. She was two hours early when she arrived at the Greyhound stop in a little shopping arcade with a windmill feature as part of the design. She got out of the car, thanked him and paid for the trip.

There were other people at the bus stop, all wearing masks, but the local people going to and from the shops were mostly not wearing any. She walked to the beach to pass some time and smiled at the very fresh memory of her and her cousins enjoying themselves on the beach. She stared at the ocean for a while, as the waves rose and fell. She was in awe of the immense power before her and wondered how such a body of water could spread all the way to India and beyond, as she saw ships slowly heading out of the harbour going to only God knew where. "It doesn't make sense," she sighed to herself.

She roused herself from her reverie and walked back to the bus stop as a huge double decker Greyhound pulled into the stop. This one was going to Durban. She wondered what it was like there. After a few minutes, a second one pulled up. She showed her ticket on her phone and the man scanned it before taking her bag and stowing it in the underbelly of the beast. She walked to the take away window at the Windmill Shopping Centre and bought some chicken, a salad, soft drink and a bottle of water for the overnight journey.

The bus was not full. As usual, people would wait until the last minute before rushing back to Johannesburg. She went upstairs and chose a seat where she could have a panoramic view of the road and stars. At 7PM exactly, the engine roared into life and the beast smoothly surged forward. To her right, Beach Hotel lights were flickering; directly in front of her the beach had gone dark but she could see some lights bobbing on the ocean. The bus made a u-turn and effortlessly heaved its huge frame away from the beach. She looked at the houses around her and wondered why this area of prime property at the beach front looked so poor and shabby.

They joined the main road, went under the highway and she saw signs that reminded her of her trip to Bisho. There were signs for Stutterheim, Berlin and Frankfort. This must be the other way to get there, she mused. They were taking the N6 for Queenstown, then Aliwal North where she remembered crossing the Orange River on her way down. It was quite an impressive sight, though not as impressive as the day she had first seen the Limpopo River. She started to cough again, unscrewed the water bottle and took a few sips. She decided to eat her food while it was still warm and then stay awake as long as possible. As they reached farmland, she had the wonderful experience of seeing a golden sunset to her left and dark sky to her right. Before long, the sun set completely and the stars came out to play. She softly sang *Twinkle Twinkle Little Star* to herself and laughed before another coughing fit interrupted her. She felt tired, but she put it down to the hectic last few days. Her eyes began to droop.

Londi awoke with a start. The sun's rays streaming in to the bus directly onto her closed eyelids woke her up. They were going through the last toll gate into the city. She must have been really tired. She had taken her modest toilet bag on board with her and went down to the toilet, brushed her teeth and splashed some water on her face. Her forehead felt warm, like she was coming down with a fever, but she thought it must have been from the morning sun on her face. She made her way back to her seat as the bus passed Gold Reef City and the Joburg skyline loomed large before her. Boy, she loved this city! She noticed the huge billboards on the buildings had changed to government messages flashing *Covid-19, wear masks, wash hands, sanitise, practise social distancing!*

As they rolled in to Park Station, she wondered whether the people at the station had seen the billboards. It was a hive of activity. The people on the benches waiting to catch buses seemed to be the only ones observing social distancing. They were seated a metre apart, with some benches seats purposefully left empty, but when she rode the escalator up to the mezzanine floor there were queues everywhere, with everyone standing close to each other. People were queuing for cash at the ATMs in a narrow corridor. There were five queues in front of ATMs and a sixth snaking its way out to the exit from a pharmacy. Almost everyone was wearing a mask, but they were standing close to each other with zero social distancing.

She walked out into the car park and morning sunlight. To her right, there was a steady stream of people going towards and from the direction of the Gautrain and bus stations and then beyond to the massive apartments in town. She turned left on Rissik Street, pulling her bag behind her. Before the traffic lights, she turned right and cut across open ground to head to the taxi rank. She was quite impressed by what she saw. Orderly queues were the norm, but there was social distancing and also a marshal, spraying people's hands with sanitiser and only two people allowed per bench in the taxi. The taxi people looked organised.

"Wow, how did the government convince you guys to follow the law!"

"*Hawu, wena Sisi,* don't be *tshatshalag*!" the tout mock threatened her. She was glad to be back in a town where she spoke a different lingo and the pulse was completely different. Despite all the crime and danger lurking everywhere, she would rather be here in the rattle and hum, mixing with gangster types, people trying to make an honest living, drunkards, lovers and church conmen, than in Butterworth, where people spoke politely and in grammatically complete sentences. She laughed gaily.

"Where are you going?"

"Alex."

"Okay. Show me your hands." Squirt, squirt! "Go in, middle bench on the far right. Keep your mask on, no touching even if I know you want me…"

She burst out laughing again. It was good to be back. Within minutes, the taxi drove out of the rank, destination Alex. As they wound through Braamfontein, Londi was surprised at how empty it was. She had left before the lockdown and, despite the knowledge that there was one, the sight of the empty streets still took her breath momentarily away. It was like the difference between knowing that sea water was salty and actually tasting sea water.

Braamfontein was normally a riot of sound, colour, funky hairstyles, students with headphones on, a cacophony of taxis, businessmen in dark suits, hotels and pubs spilling onto the pavement, hair salons and fast food outlets competing for clients and tourists transitioning through to the Newtown Precinct.

The M1 North was similarly quiet and she had never seen the Grayston off ramp so free of traffic. They crossed over into Wynberg and the traffic began to pick up. As they swung into Alex, she was amazed at the empty streets. "Goodness! It is this quiet?"

"Yes, ever since that guy was killed by the army..."

"Someone was killed? Why?"

"For not observing lockdown..."

"Yes, but we don't know whether it was the soldiers, the police or..."

"It is not the point. Our lives don't matter here!"

The typical conversation of taxis meant everyone had their say and chimed in to any conversation at any point of their choosing. That was the accepted norm in collective taxis. Londi had first struggled with the word *taxi* when she'd arrived. Back in Zimbabwe, a taxi was a sedan and it carried one or up to three passengers travelling together from the same departure point. It was private. The public one that you rode with strangers was called a Minibus or Combi. The taxi drove past Bra Joe's, past an apartment block with every balcony sporting a bored looking man with naked fat belly, housewife or children staring vacantly down in to the street.

"Bloody hell... You mean those people spend all day up there in those crowded flats?"

"Lockdown is lockdown, Sisi. Before, you were only allowed to go shopping for groceries and you must have receipt to prove you are coming from the shops. Now, people are allowed to take a walk in the mornings until nine. So you just missed them..."

"Eish, like coming out of a prison cell for one or two hours a day? Can you imagine? A lot of those flats have ten people living in a one or two bedroom unit."

"Well, you should see the people in the shacks by the river." Londi had never ventured there ever since she came to Alex. She lived in a back room on one of the narrow streets along a taxi route. Whether she was coming from work or a club, the taxi always dropped her at her doorstep. Alex was a dangerous place but she had heard even worse stories about the informal settlement by the river.

The taxi turned onto her street and Londi briefly wondered whether she had made a mistake leaving Butterworth. She got out at her front gate. The main house's front door was closed. She made her way round to the backyard, took out her key and opened the heavy padlock on the grill securing her door and then unlocked the door. She jumped as a rat scurried off into a hole. It had eaten away at the newspaper that she'd used to block it. She stuffed in some more newspaper and made a note to look for a brick to better block the hole. Her bed creaked as she sat down. Despite having slept all the way, she felt tired and decided to take a nap. Before she could lay back, she heard the back door of the main house open and footsteps.

"Londi! Is that you?"

She got up and walked to the door. "Yes, Mama."

"Oh, my child! Welcome back!" Her landlady guffawed and gave a huge hug and a kiss on the lips. Even though she was strict about the rent coming in on time, she treated her like a daughter. Besides, Londi had never failed to pay her rent anyway. She was a model tenant who followed the rules; never played loud music, did not bring strange boys into the property, kept the place neat and clean and generally kept to herself unless she was invited for the occasional meal in the main house. She was also a well-mannered young lady who had not allowed the bright city lights of Johannesburg living make her forget her traditional upbringing.

The second tenant in the backyard was troublesome to the landlady. He was a hip hop star who constantly had violent fights with his girlfriend. They always made up when they were drunk and would sometimes entertain everyone with acapella singing when everyone was in a good mood on a Saturday afternoon. Then, at times, the landlady would threaten to kick him out because his rent was always late. "You gyrate on television with all those young girls and drive fancy cars but you don't pay your rent!" she would scream at him when she'd had enough. But she never kicked him out. She loved being landlady to a township star and boasted about him to other landladies when he was not within earshot.

The tenant in the middle was a young guy from Limpopo. He worked in one of the big banks and was trying to make his way in life. He would hide himself each time there was a protest against foreigners because he said the protesters targeted his tribe too, even though he was South African. Whenever he spoke to Londi, he advised her to study hard and become independent. He would tell her how tough it was in the bank, saying sometimes he trained young white employees on how to do the job and months later he would be reporting to them. But he was determined to make it.

The landlady enquired after Londi's family in Butterworth and her general stay there and then about the trip. Londi mentioned she was still tired from the trip and wanted to take a nap. "Eat something first," urged the landlady. "I have some leftovers from breakfast." Londi followed her in to the main house and sat at the kitchen table, grateful to be spared the effort of having to cook later. The landlady's grandchildren ran over to give her a warm hug before running back to the sitting room to continue watching cartoons.

"I know things are tough, my child, but the rent must still come in at month end, neh?"

Londi smiled. "Don't worry, Mama". She quickly changed the topic. "I hear someone was beaten to death for not following the lockdown rules?"

"Oh, my child. You know we lead meaningless lives here. Do you think this would happen in the suburbs where you work?"

Londi remained silent. She found the food tasteless but was too polite to ask for the salt.

"They say they are going to do an investigation and will let us know what happened, who did what and, maybe, how he died."

Londi still remained silent. As a foreigner, she tried not to give her opinion on local matters. It was something she was conflicted on whenever there was a protest in Alexandra Park. And sometimes the protests targeted her as a foreigner, not personally but in a blanket sort of way. She escaped the wrath of the locals, of course, because she spoke Xhosa fluently and looked the part.

It was a confusing situation for her, for though she knew she was Xhosa, she was also Zimbabwean by upbringing and had not yet changed her passport, even though the opportunity had presented itself thanks to her employers' friends' efforts at helping her find her ancestral home. Back in Zimbabwe, she knew, through the other maids, a lot of white families on their street who had claimed ancestral origin to get back their citizenship in European countries when things started going bad in the country. They had sold their houses and left in droves. Her mother had told her that some whites had started coming back after the military coup. Either things were tough in Europe or they really loved their lives in Zimbabwe because it was not improving there at all.

"Have you been in touch with your bosses?" Her landlady interrupted her thoughts.

"Pardon, Mama?"

"Are you going back to work?"

"I will let them know that I am back after my rest." Londi stood up and took the plates to the little kitchen sink and started to wash them."

"Leave it, my child. Go and rest. It is good to have you back. I will see you later."

"Thank you, Mama." Londi dried her hands with a dish towel and walked back to her room. She slumped on the bed gratefully and fell asleep.

XI

Hope

Rastaman, live up!
Bongoman, don't give up!
Congoman, live up! (Yeah)
Binghi-man don't give up!
Keep your culture
Don't be afraid of the vulture!
Grow your dreadlock
Don't be afraid of the wolf-pack!

Bob Marley – Rastaman live up

Thaba peered out of his shack. He had heard right. The horses sounded different, happier. Something had happened. He saw the owner of the stables, her two children and a man leading out four horses. His spirit soared with happiness. Horses were his life and culture and he was happy to see them out and about, even though being led on a lead rope. The government must have relaxed some rules. He bent over, scooped up his child and came out of his shack and stood up straight, stretching his back. He took a few steps towards the stream and watched, smile on his face, as the horses were taken through their paces.

"Look," he pointed to his son. "Those are our animals where we come from. One day, I will teach you how to ride." Suddenly, one of the horses reared up and broke loose from the stable hand, who fell back momentarily dazed. Something had startled it. It cantered towards the stream. Thabo put his son on the ground and called to his wife, "Tumi! Tumi!" She emerged from the shack and he simply pointed at his son and ran off towards the horse that was going berserk. He approached the horse from the left, making soothing noises and talking to it softly. The horse made eye contact with him, stamped its hoof once and calmed down. He continued speaking to it and rubbed it along its neck. The owner came running awkwardly in her knee-length boots.

"Oh, thank you, thank you so much. I thought he would go into the stream and we wouldn't catch him," she said breathlessly.

"It's okay. He just got scared by a snake, I think." Thabo replied self-consciously. "There are more snakes out in the open with less people walking around."

The lady brushed back her hair and gave him a curious look as if she were noticing him for the first time. "Do you know about horses?"

"I am a MoSotho, Madam. Horses are our life."

The stable hand caught up, still a little dazed. The lady asked him whether he was okay and she handed him the lead. He took it and led the horse away.

"Thanks again," mumbled the lady and followed her hand back towards the stables. Thaba stood and watched them leave. At one point the lady glanced back and Thaba quickly turned and walked back to his shack.

"What happened," Boitumelo asked.

"Nothing. Just a startled horse, that's all."

Across the stream, Thandi was driving into the enclosure from the shops and saw the horses being led for a walk. She walked into the house and said to her sons, "They are exercising the horses. I think we are allowed riding under level 4. Shall I call and book a ride for tomorrow, boys?" The boys were happy to spend their entire lives behind their headphones glued to computer screens, but even they felt the need for a break.

"Sure thing," they replied.

She called immediately and booked for three people. Marcus was not going to join them as he considered horse riding a bit of a ridiculous, bourgeois activity. "I have never seen so much politics as in a horse riding community," he always used to say. Thankfully, his family rode for fun and because of their proximity to the stables rather than as members of a club. It also helped Thandi relax on the weekends that she chose to ride. Otherwise, the family's favourite past time was hiking.

She told the boys it was cold meats, rolls and salad for lunch. Her phone rang and she stepped out on to the patio to take it. It was Londi indicating that she was back and asking whether she was required back at work. The government had relaxed restrictions to allow live-in domestic workers to work but from what she had seen in the neighbourhood, weary and overwhelmed middle class families were breaking the rules. She knew no one in the enclosure would report her to the authorities. They all had a good relationship going and she had seen a couple of domestic workers in the area anyway. She told Londi she could come once a week for now. She needed her help. Despite the best efforts of the family to play their part, you could tell that Londi was not there. She told Marcus that Londi would come once a week from the following week.

"Really? When did she come back into town?"

"She got back this morning."

"Okay."

He went back to reading something on his phone.

"What are you reading?"

"Arundhati Roy has a piece in the Financial Times."

"That woman is special. Please send it to me."

"I will forward it. It is in line with her stance on issues but this time on India's lockdown measures and the impact on the poor over there. It is just, just incredibly sad," said Marcus putting his phone down. "You know, we complain, as we rightly should, about things but can you imagine India, Bangladesh and places like that?

"I saw a report about people walking hundreds of kilometres on Al Jazeera."

"Yep. One woman gave birth in the middle of her journey, rested for an hour or so, picked up her baby and walked for another 160 kilometres with the newborn. These stories just make me weep."

"Do you think people like Arundhati really make a difference?"

"You know what I always say: good people cannot afford to keep quiet because the bad guys are just being themselves. Look at what Modi is doing to Muslims in India. Then there's that nutcase in Brazil, Bolsonaro. I mean, a complete lunatic! Duterte in the Philippines…"

"The one who called Barack a son of a bitch?"

"Yep, than one. A cold-blooded murderer and the world lets him get away with it. Here we have Magafuli, a nutcase who believes God will protect Tanzanians from Covid-19. How reckless is that?"

"I hear they are having secret burials at night to mask the true numbers."

"Yes, there was something reported along those lines, but I don't know whether there's any proof." Marcus paused. "The world has just gone crazy in the last few years. Trump, Boris, Orban…"

"Who is Orban?"

"The chap who refused to take in refugees from Syria. He is quietly taking dictator status in Hungary and the world is too busy to pay attention."

"Don't work yourself up. Come and help me bring the lunch out." She first went to her herb garden and walked back in with some lettuce. Marcus placed his phone on the charger and followed his wife into the kitchen. She arranged some Parma Ham on a plate with some Dutch Gouda cheese and some plain crackers and rolls. Their sons ate rolls like lawn mowers. He preferred the biscuit crackers with cheese. She took out a bottle of gherkins too and they set up on the patio and called the boys to come and eat. One of them brought a bottle of achar with him. Marcus put some African guitar music from the playlist on his phone, toyed with a gherkin in his mouth and asked the boys how the preparations for the gaming tournament was going. His wife asked him to reduce the volume. He reached for the phone, took it down one notch and back to the same level again. She did not notice. The boys talked about their preparations for the upcoming online tournament while Marcus and Thandi paid attention.

Thaba was about to take his first bite of pap when one of the squatters said there was a guy asking for him. He came out of his shack and recognised the stable hand from earlier.

"Yes…?"

"Sorry to disturb. The Madam is asking to see you."

"Why?"

"I don't know. She just asked me to come and ask you to come."

Thaba glanced back at his wife. "I'll be back just now."

"But your food will get…"

Thaba was already motioning for the stable hand to lead the way. The man set off on briskly, as he if he were late for his own lunch. Thaba followed, matching the brisk pace. He had often looked longingly at the horses as he walked along the fence of the enclosure on the side of the stream towards the shops. This time, he was on the other side of the stream and heading directly to the stables! As they got closer, the smell of horses filled his nostrils and he felt like he was walking back into his village.

There were two large properties on the land, one where he guessed the family lived and one on the right where the stable hand directed him to. He took it. This served as an office of some kind, where people came to pay to ride horses. He often saw cars coming and going and ladies and children in high boots, leggings and fancy coats of different colours riding for an hour or so before gliding away in their big SUVs. The stable hand knocked on the door and the white lady came out smiling, hand outstretched. Her hair was no longer tied up in a ponytail.

"Hello! My name is Angela Schafer."

"I am Thaba, Madam."

"No, you can call me Angela. That is how we do things around here."

"Okay, Madam… I mean Angela." They both smiled. She gave him that curious look from earlier again and said, "Follow me." They walked towards the stables and Thaba relaxed and lightened quite visibly. "These are beautiful animals. Do they have names?"

The lady looked at him and smiled. She seemed to be scanning his face each time she looked at him, as if trying to study a painting. She rattled off the names of the horses one by one as she introduced them to him. She had fourteen horses in all.

"What do you think?'

"About what, Ma… Angela?"

"I saw the way you handled that nervous horse and I came back and spoke to my husband. He agreed with me that we can offer you a job to work with the horses here."

Thaba put his hand on a wooden post to steady himself. "You want me to work with the horses?"

"Yes, we can teach you to become a trainer. I lost three workers after the lockdown. They went home to Zimbabwe to be with their families and they were given five-year bans at the border."

Thaba did not hesitate. "Thank you, Angela. I welcome the opportunity. I won't let you down."

"I know you won't. You have a wife and child? I thought I saw them over there earlier."

"Yes, I do."

"You can have one of the rooms over there. Shadreck will show it to you."

Now Thaba felt giddy. He looked at her blankly as thousands of thoughts rushed through his head. Having his son around him with the horses was more than perfect. It was as if his life were coming full circle. He heard her say that she would have someone prepare the room and he could move in with his family in a couple of hours. He heard her ask something about blankets and say something about no fires inside the room, citing the dangers of a quiet killer called carbon monoxide and then suddenly he found himself alone, out on the field between the stables and the squatter camp.

He realised he was in a daze, gathered himself and walked back to towards the stream. Everything seemed greener around him, the bird songs were more amplified, the small family of ducks on the water more graceful. Even the light sparkled differently off the water as he skipped over a couple of rocks. His life was about to change in both a financial and deeply spiritual way. His life had lost meaning, as the Johannesburg dream had turned into an existence on the edge of life – mere survival from one day to the next.

Every time he walked away from the barber shop at the end of the day, thinking of wood cutting for the evening's meal and to keep the family warm, he came across smartly dressed people his age walking into the pub at the end of the shopping centre walkway, chatting into their smart phones or among themselves. This should have been his life. That failed house burglary had been the lowest point in his life. It was not just the thought that he'd reached a point where he had to break into a property; it was the humiliating manner of the failure of the attempt that stung even more deeply. Having to receive charity after that from the people he had tried to rob seemed to be a singular and pointed rebuke from his ancestors. But now, the prospect of working with the horses gave him a renewed spark in his eye. He could almost hear his ancestors chanting from the mountains of the silver streams from back home in Lesotho and they were chanting a song of joy.

Marcus walked out to the bar area by the gazebo and poured himself a beer. It made a refreshing sound in the glass, the golden colours swirled in the setting sun as bubbles rose to the surface and he smelt the wonderful aroma as it filled the glass. He took a sip, closed his eyes and smiled.

"You should see the look on your face," laughed his wife. "Can you make me a shandy?"

"No ways! That is a waste of a beer! I can pour you a glass of red or a G and T."

"But I want a shandy…" She used the childlike tone that always worked on him when she wanted her way. But these were hard times. "Come on, Thandi, I paid a premium price for these beers and you decide you want a shandy? I can get you a non-alcoholic beer at normal price!"

She gave him a look and he crumbled and grumbled to himself. "Okay, just this once and don't even entertain the thought of another one."

"How much did you pay that guy?"

"Enough to pay off Zimbabwe's debt."

She burst out laughing as she sank in to the leather couch. The bar was positioned in such a way that it captured the setting sun in winter and summer. Marcus handed her the drink and smiled. "Nice to have a beer again," he said.

The sun's rays turned a golden yellow. The light danced on the colourful autumn leaves, giving them a picture-perfect glow. The birds were beginning to settle down. A security patrol van briefly disturbed the peace as it rumbled down the servitude on patrol. They heard the van stop and the driver exchange a few words with a man walking his dogs. Despite the increasing chill in the air, the setting sun's rays gave off some warmth. The swimming pool pump stopped running and the garden went so silent that you could almost hear the silence. At some point, it was rudely interrupted by a group of hadedas cawing defiantly against the setting sun. They made the most awful racket.

"Lousy timing, guys!" sighed Thandi. The hadedas flew away squawking, their huge wings forming shadows on the poolside patio as they soared up and right towards the servitude. They talked softly about Covid-19, her online classes and local gossip.

"What happens when the lockdown is fully lifted?"

"Either we have Armageddon with our hospitals overwhelmed or by some unexplained reason that fear passes. I mean, New York has a high population density but they are not dying like flies…"

"Well, at least black people are now aware that Covid-19 affects us all. Wait, that didn't come out right. Remember how a lot of black people were saying it does not affect us when Italy and Spain were throwing up those crazy stats…."

"You are right. The good thing is that everyone, apart from a few religious crackpots, is taking it seriously. When you see even beggars at the traffic lights wearing masks, you know the message has gotten through. Nobody can claim not to have known. In fact, I saw a report that indigenous tribes in the Amazon in Brazil are being hard hit. It doesn't help that they have a nutcase as president."

"That guy has serious issues. Do you think a vaccine will be found soon?"

"I doubt it. There's a race against time to find one, but there's a danger in the race itself."

"What do you mean?"

"Well, first there are companies that I think are putting share price before science, but also you must remember that there are steps that must be taken in terms of clinical trials that you simply cut short or cut out. I am not an expert but, from what I read, there's a good reason why they say twelve to eighteen months minimum for a vaccine to be found. And, at the end of that period of time, they can still come back and say the trials failed because there were side effects at stage x of the whole thing."

"So, you are saying we are fucked?"

"No, not all. I am saying we must focus on the science and not necessarily on the hype of the hope."

"Do you think you will get paid this month?" Thandi abruptly changed the subject.

Marcus sighed, poured himself another beer and said, "I don't know." He went quiet for a moment. "We applied for the payment holiday for the bond but what do we do about the bills? Then there's Londi and Dickswell. We paid them in full last month but we can't afford to this month. So, either we pay them half each or nothing at all. I just don't know!" Marcus and Thandi loved their maid, who had been with them literally since their sons were born. It didn't help that she had moved out and had rent to pay, but they understood why. Dickswell, the gardener, worked twice a week and he too had not been coming to work because of the lockdown. He sighed again. "This whole thing is a mess."

"Stop sighing so much. We are still alive and have a lot to look forward to."

"Yep, but we will have to decide what we pay and don't pay. There's no football, so we can skip DSTV. We have to pay for Wifi, we can't ignore electricity and water. We can skip security, they take too long to respond when the alarm goes off anyway! And we can also skip the pension and investment thing."

"Have they replied yet?"

"Nope, same as the bank for the bond. We will simply not pay. If the money is not there, it is not there." He stopped himself from sighing and changed the topic. "At what time are you going riding tomorrow?"

"I booked for ten." She smiled. "It will be funny riding with masks on."

"Outlaws! Maybe I should ride in from the sunrise like a good sheriff and take you all down."

"And will you put me in handcuffs and wave your big gun around?" she asked slyly. They laughed. Twenty-seven years of marriage and the humour had not died. He turned up the music

"Do you want to dance, madam?"

They slowly shuffled to Hugh Masekela's *Market Place*.

"Please come with us tomorrow," she murmured. "You can just walk or watch us ride…"

"I will join you later. I have organised for a guy to come and cut my hair straight after breakfast."

"Is it allowed?"

"These guys are in trouble. If we can allow a customer to pay for groceries to a till operator wearing a mask, why can't a barber come to the house and cut my hair while wearing a mask? It is not like the customers in a supermarket walk one metre apart in the aisles"

It was Thandi's turn to sigh. "Don't worry," he told her. "I will be discreet. And besides, it is not like he will stay for more than half an hour. I will drop him off at the bus stop and then come and watch you guys ride."

XII

Celebration

Turn your lights down low
And pull your window curtains
Oh, let Jah moon come shining in
Into our life again
Sayin' ooh, it's been a long, long (long, long, long, long) time
I kept this message for you, girl
But it seems I was never on time
Still I wanna get through to you, girlie
On time, on time
I want to give you some love (good, good lovin')

BOB MARLEY – TURN YOUR LIGHTS DOWN LOW

Mlibo was in the mood to celebrate. He had sold his entire stash of booze, leaving only a couple of bottles of wine and ciders. His bank account looked good and he was itching to take Babalwa out to celebrate.

"But all the restaurants are closed!" Babalwa whined, flapping her arms from the elbow up and down like a chicken and stamping her feet at the same time, pretending to be a child. Mlibo smiled indulgently and drew her close to him, holding her around the small of her waist.

"I have an idea. Have you ever been horse riding?"

"Of course! We have horses in Lusiksiki. We used to ride as kids, but it was mostly the boys."

"Well, I spotted a horse riding place in Twinstreams this afternoon and I called them and booked for ten o'clock tomorrow."

"What were you doing in Twinstreams? Weren't you at the hospital?"

"I was, but instead of taking the N1 North to come back, I decided to have a look around and took the Golden Highway towards the CBD and then the M1 North. I off ramped at Rivonia onto Witkoppen and came up Witkoppen. That's when I saw the sign and called them. I felt sorry for you cooped up in here for twenty-one days."

"How very thoughtful of you babe, but I don't have those fancy riding clothes!"

"No worries. They are allowing the sale of winter clothes, so we can go to the mall now and pick up some stuff."

"You're such a darling!" she whooped and kissed him. He picked up his keys and they left the house.

The Mall looked like a strange place with everyone wearing masks.

"I guess this is the new normal," Babalwa said. "It just looks crazy!"

"I have seen one or two people without a mask," replied Mlibo.

"Really?"

"Yep."

"No ways!"

"Okay, let's see who will be the first to spot someone without a mask or wearing it under their chin. Some people forget to put it on when they get out of their cars."

The two rode the escalator to the top floor and walked hand in hand towards a clothing store, where Babalwa selected a red riding coat, brown pants and boots.

"I want to look like those ladies on TV!" she said. The lady in the shop laughed with her and glanced at her enviously. She briefly locked eyes with Mlibo as he paid but he either didn't notice or was having none of it. They walked out of the shop and headed back to the car.

"Why don't we take a drive out of town, not too far, just to get some air?" suggested Mlibo.

"Okay!" Babalwa was thrilled. Mlibo was several notches over her boyfriend, with whom she had already decided she was going to break up. Mlibo was thoughtful, polite and kind. They drove out of the mall and cruised down Cedar drive heading past Broadacres out Hartebeespoort way. There was almost no traffic on the road and it felt good to be out there in wide open spaces. They drove slowly for about fifteen minutes before turning towards Kromdraai towards the Cradle of Mankind. They encountered a few cyclists dressed in their skinny outfits, backs bent over, concentrating on pushing body to the limit. Some rode in a leisurely manner.

Mlibo pointed out places of interest he had been to as they drove along. He told her about the Cradle restaurant, showed her the Lion

Park and said there was a beautiful place hidden behind a line of trees, called Nirox Sculpture Park, where different artistes took up residence, produced great sculptures, held music concerts and where very good food was served.

"Will you bring me here after lockdown?"

"Sure thing."

She smiled. Life was good.

XIII

Glad that I live am I

Sun is shining, the weather is sweet
Make you want to move your dancing feet
To the rescue, here I am
Want you to know ya, can you understand
When the morning gather the rainbow
Want you to know I'm a rainbow too
To the rescue here I am
Want you to know ya,
Can you, can you, can you understand

BOB MARLEY – SUN IS SHINING

Londi awoke with a start. Her pillow was wet and she felt like she had a fever. She walked over to the corner of her room and poured some cold water into a dish. She splashed some water on her face and briefly shivered at the contact. She repeated the action until she felt awake and refreshed. She went outside and knocked on the door to the communal shower for the people who rented the back rooms. There was no one inside. She let the water run for a bit until it got warm. She stepped in, brushed her teeth and quickly stepped under the warm water. The landlady didn't like it when they took too long in the shower. She showered quickly, dried herself, made sure the place was as clean as she'd found it, wrapped a towel around herself and went back to her room. She dressed and picked up her phone.

"Hello, Mama," she said in the sing song voice she used when she spoke to her employer. Thandi smiled. She was happy to hear Londi's voice.

"Londi, welcome back!"

"I know I can come back to work on Monday, but if you need help I can come today."

Thandi looked over at her husband and put her hand over the piece. "Londi is back", she announced. "You are going back to work on Monday, she can do some laundry and ironing today, what do you think?" He gave a thumbs up from where he lay in the bed.

"Yes, that would be nice, Londi. I don't know whether there are any taxis on the roads. Let me know when you are on your way."

"Okay, Mama."

In Lonehill, Babalwa and Mlibo rolled out of bed, showered together, dressed and went to make breakfast together. Babalwa was in seventh heaven and was convinced she had won his heart over the last three weeks. His calls to his girlfriend had been fewer and fewer, but she couldn't tell whether he called her when he went on his hospital runs. As a rule, she was a woman who never, ever went through her lover's phone. It is something she considered anathema, reasoning that, if you went looking for bad news, you would find it. She didn't know any woman who perused her man's phone and was happy at the same time. She was not interested in playing detective. They had a light breakfast and then prepared to leave.

Londi walked out of the gate onto the street and craned her neck to see whether there were any taxis. The road was empty, bar a couple of women sweeping their front yards. The sun was shining brightly for an autumn day. Johannesburg always started her winters in fits and starts. She waited an hour before a taxi appeared. Normally, she would wait a mere five minutes and she would be on her way. She hopped on and the taxi made its way slowly through Alex, looking for more passengers. The driver did not want to get to the M1 highway without additional passengers. It was tough enough not being allowed to fill up completely, because of government's social distancing measures. He parked along the busiest street in Alex, near Bra Joe's butchery, waiting for more people to pitch up. Londi sighed quietly and exchanged WhatsApp messages with her cousins, telling them she had travelled well had rested the previous day but was still feeling a little tired.

At the stables, Thaba had already been up for a couple of hours. His wife had not seen him so happy since they had arrived in Johannesburg. He had the old spring in his step back and his eyes were sparkling like the mountain streams back home. He even whistled a tune when he worked with the horses and they seemed to all take to him. There was a group of riders coming that morning and Thaba had told Boitumelo he would get a quick bite to eat just before they arrived. He had to get his beloved horses ready.

Thandi asked the boys to help with breakfast and they readily settled on cereal and milk, arguing they would probably need a proper meal after the ride rather than before it. They loaded the dishwasher after they finished eating and the phone rang soon after. It was the barber at the gate. Marcus asked one of his sons to let him in while he went to the garage to fetch some old newspapers for the floor. He arranged them in a large square on the patio and placed a chair in the middle.

The barber walked in and greeted him in French. He was an Algerian guy who ran the barber shop at the local shopping centre. He always seemed to have new brothers and cousins arriving from Algiers or Paris. They would learn the trade in his shop and be sent off somewhere to open a new shop. He didn't talk much and they really only ever talked about football and Zidane. The longest conversation Marcus ever had with him was when Algeria won the Africa Cup of Nations.

They greeted each other and the barber asked for an extension cable, connected his clippers and started to work. About five minutes in, Thandi came out to announce that they were leaving for the stables and Marcus nodded and winked at her. She left with the boys while the barber finished with Marcus. After another fifteen minutes, Marcus was scooping up the newspapers with his discarded hair on and placing them in the bin. He opened the gate for the barber and drove out of the enclosure behind him.

Londi got out of the taxi at Sports Road instead of Broadlands Road. She walked along the road towards the stables. Her employer had asked her to pick up the keys from there instead of under the flower pot where she normally left them. The attempted break-in had sufficiently scared her to temporarily stop that arrangement for whenever they were not home. Londi walked slowly. She was losing her breath as she walked. All that eating and drinking with no exercise in Butterworth, she thought to herself.

Suddenly, she saw her employer's Land Rover pass her and stop. It reversed back to her and Marcus motioned to her to get in.

"Hello, Londi, welcome back."

"Hi, Sir…" She hardly conversed with him except when he asked about protest action in the township, her birthday or a taxi strike. But she knew he was just as fond of her as Thandi because, each time there was a problem, he would get involved and ask about it with real concern.

"How was Butterworth?"

"It was good, thanks."

"Are the people respecting the lockdown?

"No, not really, but the streets are not as busy as usual."

She put on her seatbelt as he explained why they had not left the key under the flower pot as usual. He told her about the attempted break in as they drove towards the stables. She coughed a few times but settled herself. They drove past Twinstreams Recreational Club and then Marcus parked just outside the stables. "Here we are."

They got out of the car and walked into the riding school. Thandi and the boys gave her a warm hug and Thandi gave her the key to the house as well as the small gate in the enclosure fence that gave access to the green belt. Londi took the keys and walked off into the green belt while the family prepared to go on the ride. As she walked out, another car arrived and a young couple got out.

Marcus recognised the young guy who had delivered booze to him.

"This is a small world…."

"Hello, Sir. I thought we would take advantage of the relaxed restrictions to enjoy the outdoors…"

He introduced Babalwa and Marcus introduced his family and then the riding instructor took over, introducing the stable hands who would accompany them on their ride. Thaba felt nervous. He recognised the Land Rover guy and his wife, who looked at him briefly before looking away. Thandi did not appear to notice anything and so he relaxed after a bit. Before they could mount, they heard someone running to the stables. It was a man from the squatter camp.

"Help, please! There's a young lady who has collapsed over there."

"Londi!" cried Thandi as she started to run towards the green belt.

"Wait, I am a doctor," said Mlibo. He ran to his car, grabbed his stethoscope and ran with Marcus, following Thaba and the man who had raised the alarm, to the stream. Thandi and the boys quickly followed behind. It was Londi. They recognised her coat from afar. They ran faster. Their first thought was she had slipped and fallen while trying to find the best place to cross the stream.

Thaba reached her first. She was lying inert and he knelt down to put his ear to her heart, to check whether it was still beating. Seconds later, Mlibo arrived and knelt to check her pulse. Marcus called her name and she opened her eyes, had a coughing spasm and then went quiet. Her chest was heaving as if she were struggling to breathe. Mlibo placed the back of his hand on her forehead.

"Stay back!"

Mlibo waved everyone away as Thandi and the boys caught up. He fixed his mask back on properly. He had removed it on one side because it was awkward to run with it on. He felt her temperature and a fear came over him. "Call an ambulance."

"Sorry? Pardon?"

He lowered his mask from his nose and mouth. "Call an ambulance! Quickly!"